THE TERRORIST

Also by Peter Steiner

Le Crime
L'Assassin

THE TERRORIST

Peter Steiner

MINOTAUR BOOKS

A THOMAS DUNNE BOOK

New York

This is a work of fiction. All of the characters, organizations, and events portrayed in this novel are either products of the author's imagination or are used fictitiously.

A THOMAS DUNNE BOOK FOR MINOTAUR BOOKS.
An imprint of St. Martin's Publishing Group.

www.thomasdunnebooks.com
www.minotaurbooks.com

Library of Congress Cataloging-in-Publication Data

Steiner, Peter, 1940–
    The terrorist / Peter Steiner.
        p. cm.
    "Thomas Dunne books."
    ISBN 978-0-312-37344-3
    1. Morgon, Louis (Fictitious character)—Fiction.   2. Missing persons—Fiction.   3. Students—United States—Fiction.   4. Terrorism—Prevention—Fiction.   5. French—United States—Fiction.   I. Title.
    PS3619.T4763T47 2010
    813'.6—dc22

                                                        2009047489

First Edition: June 2010

10 9 8 7 6 5 4 3 2 1

For Jane

THE TERRORIST

1

The velocity concerns me," said the doctor. He looked past his patient and out the window onto the square. It was lunchtime. The doctor was hungry. Four tables were set in front of the Hôtel de France, and two already had customers at them. The doctor said it again. "The velocity concerns me."

"Velocity," said the patient. He—Louis Morgon—said it with what could have been a sneer.

The doctor—François Verrier—looked at the paper on the desk in front of him. "There's been an increase in your numbers from the last test to this one. Not by a lot. But enough to be concerned."

"It's an unreliable test," said Louis.

"The lab in Tours is excellent."

"Don't try to distract me," said Louis. "The *test* is unreliable."

"The numbers are suggestive," said François. He removed his glasses and rubbed his eyes. He thought he could smell steak cooking.

"So what do the numbers suggest?" said Louis.

"They suggest that you should see a urologist. Just to be on the safe side. There's an excellent man in Tours." François began writing on a pad. "You don't want to play around with cancer."

"You think I have cancer," said Louis.

"As I said, the numbers are suggestive."

"I'm familiar with that kind of thinking," said Louis.

"What?" said François. He put down his pen and scowled at Louis. "If you think you know so much about it, why did you come see me? Why don't you cure yourself?"

"Cure myself of what? I came to see you because you take time to argue with me. Anyway, *you're* the physician. Aren't *I* supposed to tell *you* to heal *your*self?"

"Listen, Louis. You're seventy."

"Seventy-one."

"Your PSA levels were already high, and they just went up. Something is going on with your prostate that is worth looking at. I know better than you how unreliable the tests are. I also know that prostate cancer, if it's caught early, has a high cure rate. I also know—"

"Listen, François," said Louis. "Back in Washington, many years ago, when I was a spy—"

"What?" said the doctor. A couple was sitting down at the third table. Only one table left. Then he'd have to eat inside.

"When I was a spy—"

"When you were a spy?"

"It was a long time ago. Forty years. Before I was in Saint Leon. You were still a little boy. The people I worked with—"

"Were you really a spy?"

"You see? This is why I never bring it up. Anyway, the people I worked with—those over me and under me too— had this great and sometimes fatal propensity. They would come upon some 'suggestive' fact and then draw a conclusion from it. Then that conclusion would itself become a fact in their mind on which they would build an entire course of action."

"What on earth are you talking about, Louis?"

"I'm talking about the medical profession, François. The evidence that the sun causes melanoma is—" said Louis.

François sighed. "I see. Okay. It's very weak, you're right, but—"

"And yet," said Louis, "the dermatologist, *your* dermatologist, after cutting out my melanoma, advised me to stay out of the sun. Meanwhile the Académie Nationale de Médecine was advising everyone to forget such advice because there is an epidemic of vitamin D deficiency because everyone has been protecting themselves from the sun. You get the idea. And I won't even go into the whole cholesterol debate."

"Thank God," said François. "And why are you giving me this lecture on the vagaries and sins of modern medicine?"

"I'm explaining why I am not going to see your urologist in Tours."

"Louis, please. Prostate cancer kills many tens of thousands in France every year."

"Here's what I *will* agree to do, François. Like you, I will continue eating good food and drinking good wine." François was gazing longingly at the last table in front of the hotel. "I especially love the *moules frites* at the Hôtel de France. In fact they have a lovely Muscadet that is perfect with it. Montrésor, I think. *And,*" he said, "I will continue taking long walks. Which, by the way, is something I highly recommend for you. Then I will come back in six months to be retested . . ."

François made one last try. He slid the paper with the urologist's name across his desk. "I think you should see the urologist."

"I know you do," said Louis.

François sighed. "Four months," he said.

"Four months then," said Louis. "I'm not unreasonable. I'll come back in four months. Then we can talk about the whole 'velocity' thing."

"I can't wait." The last table was still empty. François stood up.

Louis stood up. He and François shook hands.

"Were you really a spy?" said François.

"Of course not," said Louis. "Don't be so gullible."

"Deliver the warning," said Moamar. "Go on, Father. Tell him."

"Please, Moamar," said Samad. "Wait a little. He has only just arrived."

Louis, Samad, and Moamar sat on cushions in the courtyard of the Hôtel de Boufa in old Algiers. Flames flickered in the oil lamps, and the men's shadows danced across the ceiling.

"Warning?" said Louis. "What warning?" He had already been warned this morning by his doctor. And now, no more than eight hours after François Verrier had taken the last bite of a too-small exemplar of the Hôtel de France's excellent chestnut mousse, Louis was being warned again. "I have had enough warnings for one day," said Louis.

"Well," said Samad with a shrug, "my son thinks I should warn you."

Louis held up the tiny glass filled with crimson liqueur. "First tell me what we are drinking."

"It is pomegranate brandy," said Samad. "Made by Moamar."

Louis raised his glass. "To you, my two friends. It is wonderful to be back."

"And welcome back to the Boufa," said Samad. "Your

home away from home." Samad was the hotel's proprietor. He and Louis had been friends for nearly forty years, since Louis's CIA days. Samad smiled, and his gold teeth flashed.

Louis turned as best he could and raised his glass again. "Your brandy is delicious, Moamar." Moamar had turned his back on them and was squatting over a small heap of glowing coals. He lifted the lid off the *tajine* and stirred the stew.

"Forgive my son," said Samad. "He worries about me."

"Then he is a good son," said Louis. He took another sip.

Moamar carried the *tajine* to where the two men sat and set it on the low brass table between them. A few glowing embers clung to the clay pot. They sizzled and popped as they hit the table's damp surface. Moamar lifted the cone-shaped lid, and the aromas of the stew enveloped them. Samad and Louis took turns naming the smells. "Lamb," said Samad. His eyes were closed, and his nose was raised into the air.

"And onions," said Louis.

"Yes, onions. And peppers."

"And rosemary."

"Carrots."

"Don't forget turmeric."

"Oh, yes, turmeric."

"And danger," said Moamar. "Don't forget danger. Always an ingredient in any Algerian stew."

"Let's eat before it gets cold," said Samad. He took a piece of flat bread from the basket and scooped up some of the stew.

Louis and Moamar followed suit. "And saffron, of course,"

said Louis. "It's wonderful, Moamar. I love your father. But it is your cooking that brings me back to Algiers and the Boufa. If you want me to find another hotel, then stop cooking so well."

Despite his effort to look fierce, Moamar finally let a smile sneak around the corners of his mouth. He poured three glasses of red wine from a pitcher. "To life," he said, and lifted his glass.

Samad and Louis raised their glasses. "To life."

"Including its dangers," said Louis. "Now. What is your warning?"

"A man was here," said Moamar.

"A man."

"An American."

"Ah," said Louis. "I see."

"You were our first American, when you and I were young," said Samad, "and Moamar was not yet born. This man was the second."

"His name was Phillip Dimitrius," said Moamar. "A Greek name, but he is American."

"When?" said Louis.

"Two months ago. Since your last visit."

"It could be a coincidence," said Louis.

"It probably is," said Samad.

"Another American was bound to find his way here eventually," said Louis.

"That is almost certain," said Samad. "The laws of probability."

"Another CIA man?" said Moamar.

"We don't know that," said Samad.

"He stayed three nights," said Moamar. "He was out all day every day. When I went to make his bed each morning, his room was empty, except for his toiletries, which were all in their kit, and his clothes in the wardrobe. Nothing else."

"There are people like that," said Samad. "Fastidious. Compulsive."

"No books, no papers, no newspapers, no airline boarding pass, no airline tickets, no old bus tickets, nothing in his pockets—"

"You went through his pockets?" said Samad. "Really, Moamar . . ."

"It happens in the finest hotels," said Louis.

"And nothing in the wastebasket," said Moamar. "When he left for the last time, the wastebasket in his room was still empty. What kind of person never throws any paper away?"

"A careless spy," said Samad.

Louis laughed.

"He paid cash for his room," said Moamar. "And there's this." He stepped to the desk and brought back the registry. "Look how he signed."

"Phillip Dimitrius."

"Not the name. The signature. It's like a schoolboy's signature. You can read every letter. It's too . . . careful, too practiced."

Louis studied Moamar.

"You think I'm imagining things," said Moamar.

"On the contrary," said Louis. "I think you're very good at noticing things." Louis considered for a moment. "And why do you think he was here?"

"To do research," said Moamar.

Samad nodded his head and echoed his son. "Research."

"Research on what?" said Louis.

"Research on you," said Samad. "Algiers and the Boufa—a good place to learn about you. Especially now that you have been coming more frequently. This is your fourth visit in . . ."

"Three years," said Moamar. "And here he can learn about the long-ago you as well."

"Is it?" said Louis. "My fourth visit?"

"In three years. To see the boy," said Moamar.

"That is true. And to see you both." But Moamar was right. It was mainly to see the boy.

The boy, Zaharia Lefort, had no parents. His mother, Sabiha, a drug addict and prostitute, was lost to him in the slums of Algiers. And three years earlier Zaharia had watched in a Marseille hotel as his father's throat was cut. Barely thirteen at the time, Zaharia had fled across the whole of France. Louis had taken him in and rescued him.

Given the horrors Zaharia had lived through, he should have turned out badly. But he hadn't. He now lived with his father's mother, Camille Lefort, in a small villa high above the port of Algiers. Zaharia got high marks in school. He was first in his class in history and mathematics. He was learning

English and French, and wrote Louis letters in a fine and careful hand. He was even talking about going to school in the United States.

Louis had helped Zaharia make a connection with a private school just outside Washington, D.C., which offered scholarships to deserving foreign students. Louis's daughter, Jennifer, offered Zaharia a room. "He's a really nice kid," she said on the phone. "I'd love to see him again. He should get this chance. And I've got an extra bedroom."

"Are you sure, Jenny? That's a very generous thing to do."

"Really, Dad. There's even a Potomac School bus that picks kids up in the city," she said. "If he gets the scholarship, consider it done."

Zaharia wrote Jennifer a letter.

Dear Jennifer,

Louis wrote me about your generous offer for me to stay with you if I come to Washington to the Potomac School. I am very grateful for your offer. You have always been very kind to me. I don't think I can ever repay you. If I am accepted by Potomac School, I will be happy to stay in your apartment. Thank you very much.

Sincerely, your friend,
Zaharia Lefort

Zaharia was accepted at the Potomac School.

"The next time you visit me," he told Louis proudly, "it will be in Washington. You'll come, won't you?"

"Of course I will," said Louis. "I'll go to Washington to see Michael and Jennifer, and I'll visit you too. We'll have a wonderful time." They were sitting in Zaharia's grandmother's garden sipping from tall glasses of lemonade.

"You took Pierre from me," said Camille, "and now you're taking my grandson." She rose and shook her fist at Louis. She still blamed Louis for her son's death in Marseille. "If Pierre had not left as *you* told him to, he would not have died," Camille said, "and Zaharia would still have his father." She trembled, and tears rolled from her eyes.

It was not true of course. And Camille knew it was not true. It had been the grand criminal conspiracy Pierre was mixed up in, and not Louis, that had gotten Pierre killed. But now that Zaharia was going to Washington, the anguish of her son's death rose in Camille again and caused her old bitterness toward Louis to well up. She left Louis and Zaharia alone in the garden and went inside.

"I'm going home tomorrow," said Louis finally.

Zaharia did not speak. His forehead was furrowed in thought. "Do you think I should stay here with Granny?" he said. "Or should I go to school in America?"

"That is hard for me to say," said Louis. "What do you think?"

"She likes it that I am a good student. She says she's proud of me."

"I'm sure that's true," said Louis.

"She wants me to keep learning. To go to university. I think she wants me to go to America, even though it's hard for her. She's afraid of being without me. She doesn't like being alone."

"That's certainly true," said Louis. "Nobody likes being alone."

"I'll write to her all the time," said Zaharia. "I'm good at writing letters."

"You *are* good at writing letters. Remind her of that. And you can call her on the telephone from Washington."

"Can I? Maybe Granny can come visit me in Washington," said Zaharia. His face brightened.

"Maybe," said Louis. "Tell her that too."

The next morning a cab waited in front of the Boufa while Louis said his farewells. "Room six is always waiting for you," said Samad.

"Be careful," said Moamar.

Louis embraced one and then the other. The driver pulled away from the curb. "The airport?" he said.

"I have changed my mind," said Louis. "Take me to the train station." At the station, Louis paid the fare and waited for the cab to drive off.

He got in another cab. "The Hôtel Grand Alger," he said. At the hotel, a doorman in red livery held the door. At the desk Louis asked for Mr. Phillip Dimitrius. The clerk looked up and down the ledger but found no Phillip Dimitrius. "An American," said Louis. "I believe he is a regular guest."

"No, I'm sorry, monsieur, but there is no Phillip Dimitrius registered."

"I must have missed him then," said Louis. "Do you think I could leave him a message in case he shows up?"

The clerk looked up and down the ledger again. "I'm sorry, monsieur, but I do not see any reservations for a Mr. Dimitrius."

"Phillip Dimitrius."

"No, monsieur. I'm very sorry."

Louis sat at a small table in the lobby and drank a cup of tea. The waiter brought him a newspaper. Louis watched the comings and goings. Forty years earlier, when Louis had been a spy, he had stayed here sometimes. He preferred life at Samad's Hôtel de Boufa. But the Grand Alger served a different purpose.

The Grand Alger had been frequented by the members of various intelligence services since before the Second World War. Algiers had been, and still was, a hub of espionage activity. And there had been no better place in all Algiers to gather information on allies and enemies alike than the Grand Alger, the spy hotel. From the looks of it, there was still plenty going on.

Louis watched the comings and goings. When the clerks had changed shifts he approached the desk again. "Good afternoon, sir," said the clerk. "Checking in?"

"Yes," said Louis.

"Your reservation is under what name, sir?" said the young clerk, his pen poised above the ledger.

"Coburn," said Louis. "Louis Coburn."

It was a large corner room with a view of the harbor and the Jetée du Nord. Louis hung his clothes in the closet and put his toiletries in the bathroom. He kept a small duffel with him and left the room.

The doorman summoned a cab and opened the door. "Have a nice afternoon, sir," he said.

Louis got into the cab and gave the driver an address. The man looked at Louis in the rearview mirror. He made a doubtful face. "That's right," said Louis. "Let's go."

"*Oui, monsieur,*" said the driver. "If you say so." They drove the boulevards along the waterfront—Baudin, Carnot—and then turned uphill. The streets narrowed. The buildings became shabbier. Glass was missing from windows. Trash littered the sidewalks and streets. Groups of men stood about watching who passed. The driver glanced in the mirror again. "Keep going," said Louis.

The driver drove slowly up a street of ruined buildings and stopped in front of a two-story stucco house. The first floor had once been a shop. Stained and ragged bedsheets had been nailed up in place of curtains inside the shop windows. Two plastic pots containing the remains of plants sat in one window. A skinny cat with tattered ears slept in the other window among the tiny corpses of hundreds of flies. The cat opened one eye as Louis surveyed the building.

A group of young men across the street watched Louis get

out of the cab. "Wait for me," said Louis. "I won't be long." He knocked on the door. He waited a bit, then knocked again. The door was opened by a man of thirty or so in a Lakers T-shirt and blue jeans.

"I'm looking for Sabiha," said Louis.

"Show me your money," said the man.

"It's not like that. I need to talk to her. About her son. Like last time."

The man looked at Louis for a long moment, trying to remember. "Is five minutes enough?"

"I need to talk to her," said Louis.

"Talk or fuck. It's still twenty euros," said the man, "or thirty dollars."

Louis gave the man twenty euros. "Hey!" shouted the man into the darkness behind him. "You ready? . . . Okay," he said to Louis. "Go on up."

Louis climbed the grimy wooden stairs. They creaked with every step. The walls were caked with dirt. The stairwell stunk. In the dim light at the top of the stairs stood a woman with her dress unbuttoned so that her breasts showed. She had blond hair with dark roots showing, and a pretty face. She leaned against the wall with one hand on her hip. She rubbed her breasts with the other hand.

"No, Sabiha," said Louis. "Not that. It's me, Louis Morgon."

"Oh, God," said Sabiha. She pulled her dress closed. "I'm sorry, Monsieur Morgon. Oh, please, forgive me. Please. I'm sorry . . ." She took his hand and tried to kiss it, but Louis pulled it away.

"I've just seen Zaharia," said Louis. "I wanted to tell you how well he is doing."

"Praise be to Allah," she said. "And thank you, Monsieur Louis Morgon, for everything you have done for him. You are sent by Allah. You have been Zaharia's savior and his bene-factor, all thanks and praise be to Allah . . ."

Louis let her talk. When she was finished he said, "Zaharia has received a scholarship to go to school in America—"

"Scholarship?"

"It means that someone will pay his way. He can go to a fine school for a year. Maybe longer than a year. He will get a good education. It is a wonderful opportunity for him." Sabiha sang Louis's praises all over again.

Louis interrupted her. "Tell me one thing. Have you had any American guests?"

"Americans?" She was momentarily confused by the sud-den change of subject.

"It could be important," said Louis. "Try to remember. Maybe two months ago." He described Phillip Dimitrius as Moamar had described him. "A man of forty or so, balding, squinting eyes behind black-framed glasses, this tall"—Louis held his hand a head higher than his own—"heavy, with a belly and thick arms, legs, and hands."

"Yes," said Sabiha, suddenly remembering. "Yes, I remem-ber. He wanted to talk. He gave me money to talk . . . about you. He said you and he were friends. I did not tell him much. I do not know much," she said, and looked down at her feet. "He gave me fifty dollars," she whispered. "Azar does not know."

"Thank you, Sabiha," said Louis. "I will see you when I'm in Algiers again."

"Please, Monsieur Morgon, when does Zaharia go to his American school?"

"September," said Louis. "He will leave in September."

"Then I can still see him," she said. "Only from across the street at school."

"I know," said Louis.

"Can you give me some money, like the American did? He gave me fifty dollars. Can you give me fifty dollars?"

"Let me see your arms." Instead she clutched her arms to her chest. "You'll just put it into your arms. Or Azar will take it."

"Why not? The other American did. Hal did. Hal was his name. I remember now. Just fifty dollars for all the information. Please?"

Louis went downstairs and out of the building. The taxi was gone. He walked down the steep hill and down a narrow staircase. The men across the street followed him. Louis did not speed up when he saw them. He slid open the top zipper of his bag and withdrew something small and heavy and slid it into his pants pocket. He kept his hand on the object in his pocket. The group of young men stopped and went back uphill.

Louis found a taxi near the Djemaa el-Djedid Mosque. He took the glasses case out of his pocket and replaced it in the duffel. "To the Grand Alger," he said.

Louis had dinner in the hotel dining room, which still, after all these years, served a decent bouillabaisse. He had a half bottle of a nice Bordeaux.

Louis had a good night's sleep and took an early shuttle to the airport. He flew to Paris and took the fast train to Le Mans where the old Peugeot was waiting in the parking garage.

When the maid at the Grand Alger came to clean Mr. Coburn's room, she was surprised to find that he had not left anything in the room. No wrappers, no newspapers, no bus tickets, no papers of any kind. Nothing. Even the wastebasket was empty.

II

Louis was at home working in his garden—the weeds had grown furiously in his absence—when he heard a car coming up the drive. He remained on his hands and knees between the beans and the tomatoes and watched the car, a large sedan, pass by on the driveway.

The car was traveling slowly, and the driver glanced right and left. He parked behind the Peugeot and took his time getting out. Using the window as a mirror, he adjusted his necktie and patted his jacket into place. He walked toward the front door, smoothed his jacket once more, and knocked.

Louis stood up slowly. As he did, the man turned and saw him. The man raised his hand in a friendly wave. Louis walked stiffly. His knees hurt. The man strode out to meet him. "I'm looking for Louis Morgon," he said in American English. "I'm Peter Sanchez." He put out his hand.

"I'm Louis Morgon."

"I'm pleased to meet you," said Peter.

"Are you?" said Louis.

Peter laughed. "They told me you wouldn't be easy."

"Did they?" said Louis. "And 'they' would be who? Langley?"

Peter laughed again. "They would. It was my idea to come see you. *They* were not encouraging."

"You won't be too surprised then," said Louis, "if I don't invite you to stay."

"No," said Peter. "In fact, I would be surprised if you *did*. But," he continued, "I would also be surprised if you weren't curious about why I've come."

"Why have you come?"

"To ask for your help."

Peter Sanchez was a head taller than Louis, at least ten years younger, and certainly stronger. But Louis took a step toward him and scowled up into his face. "To ask for my *help*?"

"I understand your hostility. Toward the Agency, toward government, toward everyone who—"

"My *hostility*? You don't understand *anything*."

"I think I do," said Peter. "I've read the files. I know that you were criminally abused by some of our agents. You were framed for crimes you didn't commit. You had a promising career stolen from you. Then you were set upon by . . . high officials."

"Set upon. High officials is putting it nicely," said Louis.

"You were made to seem a terrorist and persecuted for it."

"Persecuted is also putting it nicely. They tried to kill me," said Louis.

"Yes," said Peter. "They tried to kill you. I know. I know the entire catalog of horrors. It is a shameful chapter in the history of the Agency. If anything, your response seems restrained. As I say, I've read the files."

"Have you? The files. Well, well."

"It isn't information that is widely shared. But it's in *our* files, in the directorate's files, yes."

"Are you Phillip Dimitrius?"

"Who? No. Why are you asking me that? Should I know that name?"

"I was just in Algiers, and a man calling himself Phillip Dimitrius seemed to be on my trail. I was just wondering whether it was you, or someone you sent."

"I have had people checking you out, but not in Algiers. And no one named Dimitrius. I wanted to know whether you could be helpful to us, and so, yes, I have been checking. Assets, liabilities. You know how it's done."

"Yes," said Louis. "That's how it's done. That's how the mischief always begins."

"Not everything that begins that way is mischief, and not all mischief begins that way," said Peter. "But you're right.

A lot of it does. I don't know who this Dimitrius is, but I will certainly find out. And once I do, I'll tell you. In fact, I'll tell you everything my people find out about you if that is what it takes to persuade you to help."

"You're talking about a lot of top-secret business," said Louis. "I'm not cleared for anything. And never could be."

Peter waved his hand.

"So the help you want from me must be *big* help," said Louis.

"It is. Big. And dangerous," said Peter.

"I'm too old for danger," said Louis.

"Not Hollywood dangerous. Real-life dangerous."

"It involves?" said Louis.

"It involves making contact with some of your old assets in the Middle East, assets you brought in and managed many years ago, assets who were lost to us once you were gone."

"Contact for what purpose?"

"To help us infiltrate certain organizations."

"Like al Qaeda," said Louis.

"Yes, for instance. But, as you must know, terrorism is more complicated than almost anyone admits. There are hundreds of groups. And since nine-eleven a lot of them call themselves al Qaeda. It's like calling yourself Elvis. But Qaeda in England might have no connection with Qaeda in Iraq, which has no connection with bin Laden's Qaeda, et cetera, et cetera. Al Qaeda is a word. And not a helpful one. That is, unless you're a terrorist group looking for recruits."

"Or a secret agency looking for 'help,' " said Louis. "What if I refuse?"

"I wouldn't blame you. You owe us nothing. You certainly owe *me* nothing. I would leave, and you would never hear from me again."

Louis refused, and Peter Sanchez got in his car and drove down the driveway.

"And so that is that?" said Isabelle Renard. It was evening, and she and her husband—everyone called him just Renard—were sitting on Louis's terrace looking out at the garden. Louis had brought out some little crackers spread with pork *rillettes,* a bottle of Chinon, and three glasses. Clouds had come up and a light rain started falling. They all leaned in under the umbrella.

"No, Isabelle," said Louis. "In Sanchez's line of work, that is never that. It's never that easy."

"Meaning?" said Renard.

"He let me know he's at the Hôtel de France for the next two nights. He wrote his cell phone number on his card." Louis slid the card to the center of the table. "He expects to hear from me, and if he doesn't, I'll hear from him. Or someone else."

"Someone else?" said Isabelle.

"Upping the ante," said Louis. "Someone less friendly. More demanding. Vague threats maybe."

"What's this other number?" said Renard. "His license number?"

"Do you mind checking?" said Louis.

Renard was the gendarme in Saint Leon. "It will be a rental car," he said.

"From where? When was it rented? By whom? That sort of thing," said Louis.

"One never really gives up that line of work, does one?" said Renard.

"Let's go inside and eat," said Louis.

With a pair of wooden forks, Louis lifted the spaghetti out of the water and put it in a big bowl. He slid a mixture of tomatoes, basil, onions, and sardines over the pasta. He splashed on some olive oil, tossed it, and set it on the table. He opened another Chinon—last year's Médard. He sliced a baguette. They sat down and ate.

"So are you going to do it?" said Renard finally.

"No!" said Isabelle. She was alarmed. "You can't. Don't do it. Why would you?"

"I don't yet know what 'it' is. I want to know more about what they want. What they admit wanting, and what they really want."

"But, Louis," said Isabelle. She was near tears. "How can you even consider it after all that they did . . ."

Louis reached across the table and took her hand. "He said I could refuse," he told her. "He said that he would leave, and I would never hear from him again. I refused, Isabelle, and he left. If I never hear from him, it would be wonderful. But these stories don't usually end that way. The best thing for now is to find out as much as I can, in order to prepare myself for whatever happens next. If nothing happens, so much the better."

"You don't trust him," said Isabelle.

"It's not a question of trust," said Louis. "I don't think of him that way, as trustworthy or untrustworthy. He may be perfectly honest. Maybe everything is as he says it is. Maybe he kept nothing from me. Maybe he really is named Peter Sanchez. It doesn't really matter. I believe he believes what he says. But his assurances and promises make no difference. And my refusal means nothing. It's not him I worry about. I don't trust the context. I don't trust . . . events."

"And what about Pauline?" said Isabelle. "What will you tell her?"

"She's in Paris," said Louis. He looked down at his hands.

"I know," said Isabelle. "Will you at least talk to her about it?"

"I don't know," said Louis. "I don't want to frighten her away."

"She has a right to know about all this. About you."

"It's only been . . . weeks since we met. Eventually. Maybe."

Early the following evening the telephone in Peter Sanchez's room at the Hôtel de France rang, and Peter picked it up.

"Mr. Sanchez, it's Louis Morgon. I would like to talk to you."

"Shall I come to your house, Louis?"

"Please call me Mr. Morgon. Just come downstairs."

"Downstairs? At the hotel?"

"Yes."

"When?"

"Right now. I'm in the dining room."

Peter Sanchez found Louis studying the menu. Louis did not stand up or offer his hand. "Please sit down," he said. Peter Sanchez began to speak, but Louis raised his hand. "I want you to listen to me before you say anything. After you hear what I have to say, my conditions, so to speak, you may not want my help any longer.

"First let me say, over the years, I have come to despise your government—our government—and particularly the secretive, clandestine part, the dark corners where manipulation and dissembling are the common currency. And not just because of the betrayal and abuse of me and my family. I despise it for its betrayal of democracy and the rule of law. I despise it for its callous and slack code of behavior, its cynical ways, and its corrupt thinking."

Peter Sanchez sat perfectly still. He held his hands folded on the crisp white tablecloth. He betrayed no surprise or discomfort. "And," Louis continued, "I despise those who participate in this corruption.

"I have learned that you are who you say you are. (There

26

are still a few people in Washington I can call.) I believe that your intentions are what you say they are. I also believe that, as terrible as American international policy and politics have become, terrorism is even worse, and maybe even more dangerous, although that is not at all certain." Peter looked down at his hands and smiled slightly.

Louis continued. "Perhaps we can have a debate another time about what I've said. But for now, I am interested in hearing more specifically what you would like me to do. As long as it is under these conditions." Louis took from his shirt pocket a piece of paper filled with handwriting. He slid it across the table and smiled. "I and a few friends worked these out last night."

"A few friends?" Peter's eyebrows lifted as he read down the list. "What is this word?"

"Unconditional," said Louis.

Peter looked up at Louis. "Fine," he said. "I agree. Do you want me to sign something?"

"You're teasing me, aren't you?" said Louis.

Peter laughed. "Let's have dinner, and I'll tell you everything." Louis took out a pen and a small notebook. Peter hesitated on seeing the notebook, but only for a moment. Then he started talking.

The next morning Louis found Renard in his office on the square across from the Hôtel de France. Peter Sanchez's rental car was nowhere to be seen. "On the way back to the airport I suppose," said Louis.

"He agreed to everything?" said Renard.

"Of course," said Louis with a wave of his hand. "Why wouldn't he? After all, what can I do if he violates our agreement?"

"Then why did you come up with conditions at all?"

"It was expected of me."

"But you don't expect that he'll adhere to them?" Renard was exasperated.

"Don't keep looking for things to be logical," said Louis. "Or legal. Forty years ago, when I was stationed briefly in Beirut, I knew a man named Abu Massad. He was the head of a fledgling democracy movement in Egypt. When I knew him, he was living in Lebanon to avoid assassination by Egyptian secret police.

"According to Sanchez, Abu Massad is still active, although now he's back in Cairo. And he has apparently evolved away from democracy and toward a more radical fundamentalist philosophy. He has contacts with known terrorists who may, in turn, have contact with bin Laden and his lieutenants"—Louis patted the pocket that held the small notebook—"if any of this is to be believed."

"You don't believe it?" said Renard.

"Sanchez is a very enterprising and serious investigator," said Louis. "He went through forty-year-old files and found that old, brief connection between me and Massad. Next— and I'm guessing here; he told me none of this—he discovered my biography. Then he looked over my list of assets from my days in the Middle East. Many are gone, or dead. But some, it turns out, are still around. Most are no longer on the CIA payroll or, for that matter, friendly to the United States, Abu Massad included. Sanchez wants me to renew my old acquaintanceships to help the Agency get as close as possible to bin Laden and others."

"Why you?" said Renard. "Why not some CIA loyalist? You're hostile to the CIA, and they're not exactly friendly toward you."

"I'm certainly not the only one they're in touch with," said Louis. "I promise you that. They're desperate, and they're trying whatever they can think of. I represent a promising avenue for them because I've got anti-American bona fides. Remember, I was once thought to be a terrorist. I can easily persuade . . . someone . . . of my hostility to the United States."

Renard looked at Louis in astonishment. "Bona fides? You were set up."

"The people I'd be meeting in Cairo or wherever it is don't know that," said Louis. "Anyway, I haven't said I'll do it."

"But you will, won't you?"

"I haven't said I will."

"But you will, won't you?"

It had been four years since Solesme Lefourier's death. Louis still averted his eyes when he drove past her house, because he knew if he looked she would not be there. A young Dutch couple had bought the house after her death. Louis had stopped by to introduce himself. They had invited him in. To his relief it was a different house inside. But that changed nothing.

Solesme remained a profound presence in Louis's mind. She came and went as she pleased. He had only to close his eyes, and there she would be walking up the driveway. He saw her laugh or frown. He saw her absently brush her hair from her eyes with the back of her hand. He saw her naked back, asymmetrical and beautiful. He even felt her body against his own. He saw her grow thin from the disease and become still more beautiful. Her skin became almost translucent. Her eyes shone. And then she was gone. Maybe it was the emptiness Solesme had left in his life that caused him to even consider the ridiculous venture Peter Sanchez proposed.

Louis dismissed the idea. "Nonsense," he said. "It's not you." He sometimes talked to Solesme. He was sitting in his kitchen looking over the notes from his conversation with Sanchez, when Solesme entered his thoughts. "What will I tell Pauline?" he said.

Solesme did not usually respond when he spoke to her. But this time she did. "Everything," she said.

"But it's only been a few weeks since we met," said Louis.

"At the Dissay flea market. I know," said Solesme. "Tell her everything."

Louis had driven over to Dissay and parked with the other cars on the mowed field at the edge of town. Louis liked flea markets. They reminded him of the markets in old Istanbul and Sarajevo and Cairo. Louis walked among the stands and crates and tables loaded with merchandise. He stopped at a makeshift stand, sagging under old tools and machine parts, odd springs and gears and bolts. He picked up a small, rusty iron box with some grooves carved into one side and a sprung lever on the opposite side.

"It's yours for three euros," said the man sitting in the

canvas lawn chair. He wore a sleeveless shirt and a cap pulled low over his eyes. He squinted as smoke from his cigarette curled up into his eye. His hair hung to his shoulders. "In fact," he said, "for you, I'll make it two fifty."

"What is it?" said Louis.

The man looked at Louis with mild disgust and turned away.

At another stand Louis looked through stacks of napkins, sheets, old lace, pillowcases. He pulled out a pair of heavy linen sheets. "They don't make bedsheets like that anymore," said the woman sitting behind the table. She stood up. She was thin and beautiful, maybe twenty-five, with coffee-colored skin and large green eyes. "I have the pillowcases that go with them," she said and began searching through the pile.

"How much is the set?" said Louis. He watched her sort through the stack. "Sheets and pillowcases."

"Twenty euros," said the young woman.

"Can we open them out?" said Louis. "So I can see the whole sheet?"

"Of course," said the young woman.

"They have to be ironed, you know." This came from another woman sitting under a linden tree. She put aside the newspaper she had been reading. "They should go to a good home," she said. "Where somebody irons. Do you iron, monsieur?" She—Pauline—stood up and stepped forward.

The younger woman rolled her eyes. "He's a customer, *maman*. Don't scare him away."

Pauline was thin, like her daughter, but not as tall. She had pale skin and red hair and the same green eyes as her daughter. She squinted in Louis's direction. "I'm not driving him away, *ma petite*. Tell her, monsieur."

"On the contrary," said Louis. "Your mother is closing the deal. You see, despite my derelict appearance, madame, I am a man"—he made a dramatic flourish with his arms—"who irons." The two women laughed.

"You see?" said Pauline.

The younger woman put the sheets and pillowcases in a paper bag. Louis gave her twenty euros.

Pauline turned to her daughter. "I am going for a walk," she said. She turned to Louis. "May I walk with you?"

"Of course," said Louis. "It would be my pleasure."

"I was getting bored just sitting there," she said.

They ambled through the flea market, stopping now and then at stands and appraising the offerings. "That is a Russian military mess kit from the Second World War," said Louis. "It would be valuable if you found the right collector."

"Really," said Pauline as though she found that fact interesting. "You are not French, are you?" she said, squinting again. She had an appraising manner, tilting her head to one side and half closing one eye, as though she were regarding suspect goods. She held her hands behind her back and her chin thrust out.

Louis looked crestfallen. "Is it that obvious? I've been here for decades, and still my French gives me away."

"But no, not at all, monsieur," said Pauline. "Your French is excellent and charming. But still you *are* a rarity in France."

"An American expatriate?" said Louis.

"Don't be silly," said Pauline with a wave of her hand. "A man who irons."

They introduced themselves.

"This is my car," said Louis. He opened the door and put the linens in the backseat.

"Perhaps I am being forward," said Pauline. "Marianne would be appalled if she heard me. But are you free for supper this evening? You see, she is making a farewell dinner for me—I'm going back to Paris tomorrow. The other guests will all be her friends. They're all young. It would be lovely to have someone my own age there. Could you come?"

Louis said that he would be honored.

He found the small cottage in the village of Villedieu-le-Château and knocked at the door. He handed Marianne a bottle of wine and a bouquet of flowers from his garden. He shook hands with everyone. Louis and Pauline sat opposite each other at the long table and let the animated sounds of young conversation sweep over them.

Pauline Vasiltschenko—the daughter of Russian immigrants—was six years younger than Louis. Marianne was her youngest child. There were also two sons. "They are all hopelessly wonderful," she said as she caressed Marianne's cheek. Marianne was a teacher. "Too little money," said Pauline.

Frank, the middle child, was a businessman. "Too much money." Anwar was a photographer. He was named after their father, a Senegalese physician living in Paris. "Their father and I are no longer together."

Louis invited Pauline to join him for a walk the next morning. "I will get you to the station in Saint Pierre in plenty of time for your train." He picked her up after breakfast and put her bag in the trunk of the old Peugeot. They drove out past the Beaumont chateau, parked beside the Dême, and started walking. After following the small, meandering river for two or three kilometers, the trail climbed a steep hillside and went through some abandoned vineyards. Only stumps remained where the vines had been. The supporting posts and wires had been overgrown and pulled over by weeds.

From the vineyard, they turned north and walked into a forest where they joined a forest road. The road was arrow straight. There was a clearing far ahead where the sunlight slanted in. At the clearing, they turned east on another forest road and then south on a path that carried them out of the forest and back down to the Dême. They passed close by the Beaumont chateau.

"That was a wonderful walk," said Pauline.

"When you're back in Villedieu," said Louis, "perhaps we can do it again."

"I expect to be back in the next week or two. I'll let you know."

"A farewell dinner, and you're back in a week or two?"

"I hadn't planned on it," said Pauline. "But now I have a reason to come more often."

"Ah," said Louis.

"For the walks," said Pauline, squinting into the light, her hands behind her back, her chin out.

"Of course," said Louis. He wondered later whether she could have divined somehow that walking was the way into his heart.

Pauline called Louis a week later. She said she was coming to Saint Leon the following Friday. "Marianne has school Friday and Saturday, so I'll be free. If you're inclined to show me another of your walks, I would love it."

Louis watched Pauline as she stepped off the train. She wore shorts, a T-shirt, a billed cap, and well-worn hiking boots. She had a small knapsack slung over one shoulder. When she caught sight of him, she smiled broadly. "What a perfect day," she said.

"I thought we would drive to La Rochcorbon," said Louis. "It's nearby. There's a walk from the village up through the vineyards, then down into Vouvray, and back along the Loire. Maybe four hours."

"Perfect," said Pauline.

After two hours, they stopped for lunch. Louis had brought along a baguette, some Gruyere, a couple of tomatoes, and some strawberries. They sat on the grass at the edge of a bluff in the shade of a chestnut tree and looked out over the rooftops of Vouvray.

"When the cheese gets this soft, if you take a bite of cheese, bread, and tomato, all at the same time, it's like a grilled cheese and tomato sandwich."

"I don't usually eat sandwiches," said Pauline.

"Really? Sandwiches are one thing I miss. Do you know what a Reuben is?" He explained what went into a Reuben sandwich.

"I'm not persuaded," said Pauline.

"I'll make you one someday. The sandwich itself will persuade you."

The strawberries were plump, and the juice ran down their chins. "Water?" said Louis. They passed the bottle back and forth.

They walked down through Vouvray, crossed the highway, and found the trail to the riverbank. Some clouds had come up, and a light rain began to fall. "What is that?" said Pauline. She stopped and cocked her head. "Music?"

"Ah, the *guinguette*," said Louis. He had forgotten about the little riverside bar. "It's Friday afternoon, maybe a little early. There might be dancing." He heard the accordion now and the strains of the *bal-musette*.

"Let's stop," said Pauline. "We can wait for the rain to pass."

The *guinguette* consisted of nothing more than a counter crowded with bottles, a portable wooden dance floor, and a couple of tables. The roof was a bright blue tarpaulin stretched between some trees. The music came from a pair of speakers beside the bar.

It was about three o'clock. Besides Louis and Pauline, there were only four other people. The bartender and a customer stood across the bar from each other. They leaned in so that their faces nearly touched. They seemed engaged in an animated, yet intimate, conversation. When one or the other raised his voice too much, they would both look around to see who had heard them and then return to whispering.

The other people, a man and a woman, were dancing. Louis and Pauline got glasses of wine at the bar and sat down at one of the tables to watch. The dancing couple were not young. She was short and thick bodied. She held her head thrust forward. She wore ugly glasses, and her gray hair was in an unbecoming style. The man was taller, but he too had a middle-aged sort of ordinariness about him. His pants bagged out at the knees. He was balding. They both wore dancing shoes that they had brought with them. Their street shoes sat at the edge of the dance floor alongside her purse and what must have been a shoe bag.

The *bal-musette* is a quick waltz, a sort of urban folk dance. It has mostly disappeared, except for at the occasional *guinguette*—*guinguettes* are also disappearing—where it lives on. Without the *musette,* the *guinguette* is not a *guinguette.*

The dancing couple leaned into one another slightly. Her right hand was raised and cupped in his left, her left arm draped on his shoulder. His right arm lay against her back lightly with his fingers relaxed, his palm down. They spun about the floor turning small circles, their legs and feet taking little hops in perfect synchronicity. And yet they glided as though they were skating. Their dance was a beautiful thing. Louis and Pauline watched in silence.

Louis invited Pauline and Marianne to his house for dinner, along with Renard and Isabelle. Louis's hair was combed, and he had put on a shirt Renard had never seen before.

Louis had made a fish stew, which everyone said was wonderful. "I have an early morning," said Marianne after dinner. She and her mother kissed the others good-bye, and they left.

Isabelle pronounced Pauline *très belle*.

Renard said she was *agréable*. Isabelle poked him, and he laughed.

Pauline called again the following week. "Come to Paris," she said. "There's a brilliant production of *The Imaginary Invalid* at the Comédie Francaise." Pauline had a spacious apartment looking out on the Jardin du Luxembourg, including a beautiful guest room with its own bath and kitchenette. "It's yours whenever you want it," she said.

After the play, Louis lay on his back with his hands behind his head. He vowed to read Molière in French. He listened to the traffic noises, the sound of laughter from the park below, the sirens coming through the tall open windows. The curtains billowed into the room. The city lights moved across the ceiling. In his dreams he saw the *guinguette* couple dancing. Except it was Solesme dancing with Pauline.

"You're still getting over someone," said Pauline the next time she was in Saint Leon. They were having a late lunch on Louis's terrace.

"Solesme Lefourier was her name," said Louis. "Except I'm not getting over her. She died. I have no intention of getting over her.

"I'm sorry," he said then. "That was unkind. It sounded harsher than I meant to be."

Pauline smiled. "You don't have to apologize. I understand love, and I understand loss."

"I'm a little fearful," said Louis.

"Of what?" said Pauline.

"Of getting over her. Of losing her, once and for all."

Pauline looked up at the sky. "Let's take a walk before it rains."

They walked down Louis's driveway. "Solesme lived right there," said Louis. He paused for a moment to look at the house. They took a grass track that crossed the Dême on a narrow stone bridge. They followed the river south this time, instead of north.

"You know," said Pauline, "you don't have to be afraid of losing Solesme."

"I also fear *not* losing her," said Louis.

Pauline laughed. Louis laughed too.

After a time, they turned onto a trail that led uphill through dark woods. At the top of the hill, they crossed some vineyards. The grapes hung in fat clusters. You could hear the armies of bees working on the grapes that had fallen to the ground. The Beaumont chateau lay below them. They came to an abandoned quarry. The water was clear and deep, and the granite walls disappeared into its blackness.

It was a sweltering day, in spite of the overcast sky. Pauline's forehead was beaded with sweat. Sweat showed on the back of her shirt. Louis could feel sweat running down his back and chest and under his arms. He took off the broad-brimmed hat he was wearing and fanned himself with it. He opened the front of his shirt. He mopped his forehead with his sleeve. They sat on a stone and gazed down into the water.

"During the War, terrible things happened here," said Louis.

"In Saint Leon?" said Pauline.

"In Saint Leon," said Louis, "and on this very spot. A Nazi officer was executed by the resistance right here."

"You know," said Pauline, "it's an odd coincidence that my daughter lives nearby. I actually passed through Saint Leon during the War. In my parents' arms, of course. I was a newborn. We were Jews. We started in Paris. We were helped by partisans. We were taken from place to place, sort of like the American Underground Railroad. When the War ended, we had made it as far as Foix, not far from the Spanish border. When I was old enough, my parents showed me our entire journey on a map. It came right through Saint Leon."

Pauline untied her shoes, took them off, then took off her socks. "Let's go swimming," she said. She did not wait for Louis to say anything. She stood up and removed her clothes.

Her body was slim and muscular. Louis watched astonished as she climbed down the rocks and slid into the water. She let out a whoop of delight and swam away from the shore. Louis took off his clothes and followed her.

"What else could I do?" he said that night as they lay in his bed.

"You know," said Pauline, "when I was a practicing physician, I saw hundreds of people naked. You would think I would have gotten used to it over time, even gotten bored looking at naked people. But I never did; I still haven't. It has always thrilled me. I never got tired of seeing my patients' bodies. It was their uniqueness, the particularities of each body that I loved. And their beauty.

"I never once had an affair with a patient. But I admired all their bodies. Secretly, of course. I had one patient who had been in a terrible street bombing. He had lost part of a leg and had wounds up and down the right side of his body. Still, I found him beautiful to look at. He was tall and thin with narrow muscles. He had pale, pale skin. His blue veins showed through everywhere. He seemed nearly transparent. Which," she said, "is why I made you take off your clothes at the quarry."

"You made me . . . ?" Louis looked doubtful.

"Of course I did," said Pauline. "Why else do you think I took off my own clothes? I knew you were too much a gentleman not to follow suit. You have an interesting and beautiful body. That is why I undressed. It was my way of undressing you."

Louis ran his hands over her shoulders and down her back. "Well, of course, that too," she said with a little shiver. "There was that."

The next Thursday, Louis met Pauline's train in Saint Pierre. He tried to take her bag. She squinted at him. "I carry my own bag," she said. "Or don't you remember?"

"I remember," said Louis. They drove in silence.

"You have something to tell me," she said.

How did she always seem to know what he was thinking? Louis drove in silence for a while before he said, "Yes, I have something to tell you." He took a deep breath. "I want to tell you about myself as a young man living in Virginia, with a young wife and two small children. Sarah was my wife, Jennifer and Michael my children. I've spoken about them before."

"Yes, you have," said Pauline. "But not much."

"No," said Louis. "I know it doesn't work this way, but not speaking of them is my way of protecting them. Or trying to. Well." He looked across at Pauline. "We lived in Arlington, Virginia, outside Washington. I was working for the State Department. My wife was smart and beautiful, my children—Jennifer and Michael—were . . . lovely."

"Say more about them," said Pauline.

Louis pulled to the side of the road and stopped the car. "As astonishing as it may seem," he said, "I did not pay much attention to them." He held the steering wheel as though he were still driving. "I sometimes held them on my lap after supper, or I played with them in the yard. But while I was pushing the swing, my mind was elsewhere—a meeting the next day, a position paper I had to write. Sometimes I would look at them playing or sleeping and wonder, *Who are these little people? What do they have to do with me?*

"Jennifer was always organizing the neighborhood children into groups to put on plays or sell lemonade. One summer she organized things so that there was a stand on nearly every corner. No adult could get home from work without passing at least one stand, and more likely several. Jennifer broke their resistance. Eventually they *had* to buy a cup of lemonade. All the children divided up the profits. How did she think to do that?

"And Michael. Michael loved to draw. He drew endlessly. Once I found him lying on his stomach on the porch drawing a dead mouse. He would squint at the tiny body, then draw, then look again. A long line of ants went from the edge of the porch to the dead mouse, and he drew the ants too. How did he even know how to do that? What was he seeing?

"I didn't ask myself—or them—any of those things I should have asked. I was young and self-absorbed. I was getting rapid promotions to good and responsible jobs. I sat in on presidential briefings. I thought I was important.

"In retrospect the briefings were mostly boring. And alarming."

"Alarming?"

"They revealed, if I had been willing to see it, how ill equipped these people were to rule the world."

"Did they rule the world?" said Pauline.

"In a manner of speaking they did," said Louis. "And I actually thought I would too. Eventually I was posted to the CIA. It was the Cold War. I was sent to Cairo, Algiers, Istanbul. I was on a fast track, I was told. I had a big career ahead of me, I was told.

"One day, I was called into the secretary of state's office. I thought I was going to be promoted." Louis laughed. "That shows how little I actually understood. Instead I was read a nasty bill of particulars accusing me of all sorts of wrongdoing. I was dismissed from the government. I was escorted from the building by guards." He paused and looked at Pauline. "I don't know how much to tell you," he said.

"Everything," said Pauline.

"Yes," said Louis. "Everything. So. I had not done any of the things I was accused of—revealing secrets, compromising operations, endangering agents. I had been sabotaged by the man who had been my mentor. His name was Hugh Bowes. He was very powerful."

"Hugh Bowes?" said Pauline. "Wasn't he the . . . ?"

"Secretary of state," said Louis. He nodded. "This was long before he was the secretary of state. But even then he was jealous of his power. Because I was ambitious, on the rise, I don't know, because of all that, he was jealous of me."

"And that made him want to ruin you?" said Pauline.

"I know," said Louis. "It sounds ridiculous. From this vantage it sounds impossible. But operating in that rarified, claustrophobic world does that to you. It unhinges you. It separates you from reality. You invent your own truths and begin believing them. Anyway, that is when my life began to unravel. My promising career was in ruins. My marriage came apart. I left my family. I came to France."

"Your children?" said Pauline.

"Yes," said Louis. "I left my children. They were small, and they needed me, and I left them. I didn't see them for years." He met Pauline's eyes.

"And what about now?" said Pauline.

"Oh, now. I see them, I write to them, I call them," said Louis. "They are wonderful—generous and loving. Far more generous and loving than I deserve."

Pauline reached across and touched his hand.

"And you moved to France," she said.

"Coming here made as much sense as anything else I could think of. I wanted to leave my past behind and start over. And I did. I bought my house, fixed it up. Saint Leon came to feel like home. There was Solesme. My friends, the Renards. And others.

"Then, not too many years ago, when I thought that sordid political world was gone forever, I came out onto my terrace one morning, carrying my breakfast tray, and almost tripped over a dead body. An African. Or so I thought. At first."

Pauline's green eyes had grown wide with astonishment.

"As I eventually discovered, Hugh Bowes, my old enemy, had arranged it. It—the dead man—was part of an elaborate scheme to do me in once and for all. My destruction had somehow—don't ask me how or why—become his obsession."

Pauline turned away from Louis. She leaned forward and peered hard through the windshield, as though she were trying to get her bearings. She looked at the fields of yellow wheat stubble in front of them, at the sunlight dancing off the winding creek, at the tractor pulling a wagon piled high with bales of hay. The bales teetered and rocked but didn't fall. She watched a flock of sparrows scatter across the sky, heard the wind rattling the poplars beside the road. This was the world as she knew it. Routine, ordinary. She turned back to Louis. "Is that all over?" she said. "Is it finished, or is it still going on?"

Louis smiled. "Hugh Bowes is dead. Several years now. Maybe it is over. But these stories don't end easily. I don't know whether it is over. What makes me bring this up now is that last week a man from the CIA calling himself Peter Sanchez showed up at my house. I had had no contact with anyone from that world for years. I didn't know he was coming. He just showed up.

"Peter Sanchez wants me to take up with some of my old contacts in Egypt. I would tell you their names, but they would mean nothing to you . . ."

"I thought such matters were state secrets, or whatever you call them," said Pauline.

"I no longer believe in such secrets. Sanchez is asking me to go on this 'mission,' and I am trying to decide whether to do it or not."

"And are you thinking this is another plot to entrap you somehow? Doesn't that seem a little . . . unlikely?"

Louis smiled. "Yes, it seems unlikely. Even to me. That's not what I'm thinking."

"Then why are you telling me all this?" said Pauline.

"Because you have a right to know about me. Because I want you to know who I am. This history I have. My history is a kind of . . . poison that's in me."

"Poison?"

"I think of it that way."

Pauline gave him a hard look. "You think your history is who you are?"

"It's *part* of who I am," said Louis.

"And will you go on their mission?" she said.

"I don't know."

"Why don't you know? Why would you do it? Can't you just decide not to do it? Just refuse to do it?" she said. "Don't you have a choice?"

"I don't know whether I have a choice. The only way to know would be to refuse to do it. And if I don't have a choice after all, then the consequences could be worse than they would have been if I had not refused."

"You mean, they would do something to force you to do whatever it is they want you to do?"

"That sort of thing happens," said Louis.

Pauline frowned while she studied Louis for a long moment. "What is the real reason you don't refuse? Just refuse . . . unless it interests you."

Louis looked down at his hands.

"That's it, isn't it?" she said. "It interests you."

"Yes," said Louis, "it interests me."

"So, does it interest you because you think it is a good thing to do? Or because it is an obligation? Or because it is an exciting adventure? Why?"

"I think it . . . *might* be a . . . *useful* thing to do."

"Useful? *Might be useful?*" Pauline was angry.

"I might find a way to get to some harmful person," said Louis. "Some terrorist, say . . ."

"In order to kill him?"

"I wouldn't do it, but someone else would. Yes, that would be the objective," said Louis.

"And how would killing him be useful?" Before Louis could answer, Pauline continued. "Wouldn't killing him just make him a martyr? Aren't there more who could easily take his place? I know it's not my area of expertise, but killing him doesn't make any sense to me."

"That is not the way the world is, Pauline." His voice had taken on a hard tone. "That kind of nuanced world is the world you *wish* we lived in. The world we actually live in is a nasty, brutal world, governed by violence and power . . ."

"I don't believe you," Pauline said. She had turned in her

seat to face him. "I don't believe you, Louis. I don't believe your reasons. I've only known you a short time. But I don't believe that is the way you think. I believe your continuing anguish at having left your children many years ago. I believe you when you say you quit that political, Hugh Bowes world because you found it confusing and treacherous and corrupt. Morally repugnant. Contemptible. Bankrupt. Those were *your* words."

IV

I have decided that I cannot help you, Mr. Sanchez."

"I understand, Mr. Morgon. I understand completely. I will not bother you again." Sanchez hung up the phone.

The summer turned into fall. Louis continued as he had before. He took long walks in the fields and forests around Saint Leon, with Pauline when she was in town, alone when she wasn't. He worked on a series of portraits he had begun of his friends. "They're strong paintings, Louis," said Isabelle.

Pauline thought so too. "You should exhibit them."

"I don't think so. Not yet, anyway," said Louis. "The trick with a portrait is to get a strong and lively likeness, and a good painting at the same time. And to know when to stop. I'm still learning when to stop. Look at Sargent's paintings." He pulled a large book of Sargent's work from the shelf, and he and Pauline sat with the book on their knees while Louis turned the pages. "Look there," he said. "One more brushstroke, and he would have killed it. That's what I have to learn."

"There's a Sargent show opening," said Pauline the next time she called. She mailed Louis the catalog. "Come up and see it. It's wonderful. A lot of things from private collections. Wonderful portraits of children."

"No one was better with children than Sargent," said Louis.

"You won't see them again," said Pauline.

"I just can't make it," said Louis. "I'm just too busy."

He saw Renard and Isabelle when he could, and other friends too. Marianne invited him for dinner. Pauline was there, of course, along with some young people Marianne thought Louis might like to meet. "A couple of them are artists," she said. "Like you." Louis enjoyed talking with them. He invited them to see his work.

"Representational art is dead," said Paolo, a young Parisian. He stood in front of Louis's canvases with his arms crossed. "It just doesn't know it."

"If it doesn't know it," said Louis, "then everything is fine."

Paolo laughed. "It's only fair that I give you a shot at my work," he said.

Paolo had made part of an old workshop on the edge of town into his studio. He constructed enormous sculptures out of old computers and televisions that he stacked in a heap, wrapped in plastic sheeting, and dribbled with tar and other industrial materials. Then he plugged everything in. The television and computer images were refracted by the coated and splattered plastic into shimmering and winking specters. "Industro-apocolyptic," said Paolo.

"I see," said Louis, sounding doubtful. Louis liked Paolo, and Paolo liked him. They met for coffee at the Hôtel de France. Louis talked about his need for color and beauty. Paolo needed energy and chaos.

"Louis finally has somebody to talk to about art," said Renard.

Pauline invited Louis to come to Paris again. And once again he didn't go.

Pauline came to Saint Leon nearly every week now. She and Louis took walks, they cooked dinners together, they sat side by side on his sagging sofa and read. One evening Pauline laid her book aside. "Louis," she said. "Tell me what is going on with you." Louis tried to continue reading, but she wouldn't let him. "Louis, what is going on?" She put her hand over where he was reading.

"Going on?" said Louis. "We're reading. Or trying to."

"We're reading," she said. "But that is not what is going on. There's something you're not telling me."

"We're having a relaxed evening."

"Stop being evasive," she said. "You skipped the Sargent show, which you know you would have loved. You didn't . . ."

"I'm waiting," he said.

"Waiting for what?" said Pauline.

"I'm waiting," he said, "for the other shoe to drop."

"The other shoe . . . ?"

Louis explained the expression to her.

A week later the other shoe dropped.

The telephone rang. "Dad," said Michael. His voice sounded panicked.

"What's wrong, Michael?"

"They've arrested Zaharia. They took him away. We don't know where."

At the Algiers airport, Zaharia Lefort had kissed his grand-mother again and again. "Don't cry, Granny," he said, "I'll write. I promise."

"I know you will," said Camille, but she only held him tighter. Tears rolled down her cheeks.

"Aren't you happy for me?" he said.

"Oh, yes. Of course I am," she said. "And very proud." She smiled up through her tears and pinched his cheek.

"I've got to go, Granny. Everybody else is on the plane." He embraced her once more and turned and walked to the gate. He turned again and waved and then was gone.

Zaharia held his face pressed against the window nearly all the way to Paris. He found his way through the corridors and gangways to the Washington Dulles flight.

The flight itself seemed endless. He had studied the flight information, so he knew exactly how many miles it was. But the ocean was bigger than he could have imagined. It went on and on, steel gray and unchanging, like a great, unblinking eye. Then finally they were flying over forested land dotted with lakes. Then there were roads. Then there were farms and cities and houses with swimming pools. Then they were on the ground.

Zaharia lined up with the non-U.S. citizens and waited behind the yellow line, as instructed. The agent signaled him forward, leafed through his passport, studied the visa, and put the open passport facedown on a scanner.

"What's the purpose of your visit?"

"I am going to school," said Zaharia.

"Are you traveling alone?"

"Yes."

"Look up here," said the agent, pointing to a small camera. The agent handed the passport back to Zaharia. "Welcome to the United States," said the agent.

Zaharia pulled his two suitcases from the carousel and walked out through the double doors. He found Jennifer in the crowd.

"Look at how tall you are," she said. "You're grown up. Oh, Zaharia, I'm so glad to see you." She put her arms around him.

He wouldn't let her carry either suitcase. "I can do it," he said.

Michael and Rosita, his wife, came for supper. Zaharia ate his first pizza.

"Here is your room, Zaharia. And here is your bathroom." Zaharia was astonished. "*My* bathroom?" he said. "Wow." Jennifer laughed.

"Where did you learn 'wow'?" said Michael.

"It's not correct?" said Zaharia.

"It's *very* correct," said Jennifer, and Zaharia grinned. "Wow," he said again.

The next morning, Zaharia boarded the bus for the Potomac School. He sat next to a Chinese boy. The boy eyed him warily.

"Are you from China?" said Zaharia.

"My grandparents," said the boy. His name was Albert Chan. "What about you? Where are you from?"

"Algiers," said Zaharia. "The capital of Algeria. My name is Zaharia Lefort."

"Algeria? Wow," said Albert.

The school's headmaster took Zaharia to his classroom and introduced him to the teacher, who introduced him to the class. "Sit right there, Zaharia," said the teacher.

Zaharia had waited his entire life for this moment. He hung on every word that every teacher said. He did every assignment, did work for extra credit, asked his teachers for more work.

"I want to be on the basket team," he told the basketball coach.

"You mean basketball. Here," said the coach, and handed Zaharia a basketball. "Let's see what you can do." The coach got into a defensive crouch.

Zaharia just looked at him. "I'm sorry, but I've never played basketball."

The coach stood up. "Well, you're big enough. But you've got to learn the game before you can be on the team." Zaharia asked Albert Chan to teach him. "I'm only here one year," he said. "I have to learn everything."

Zaharia had been at the Potomac School for two months when he was summoned to the headmaster's office. Two men, wearing dark suits and ties, stood waiting. "Zaharia Lefort?" the older one said. "Please come with us."

"Where are we going?"

"Please come with us," said the man. The men stepped to either side of Zaharia.

"Where are we going?" said Zaharia. He turned to the headmaster. "Is it all right, Mr. Korngold?"

"Yes, Zaharia. You have to go with these gentlemen." Mr. Korngold's face was ashen, his eyes were wide open as though he had just seen something terrible.

As soon as the men had taken Zaharia from his office, Mr. Korngold picked up the telephone. He dialed a number and waited. "Mr. Irelan, please. It's urgent. This is Bernard Korngold. . . . Jack? Bernie Korngold . . . Listen, Jack, some federal agents just arrived at the school . . . FBI . . . They took away one of our students. . . . Of course they had warrants. . . .

Zaharia Lefort . . . Yes, one of our international scholars. . . . They wouldn't say . . . Algeria."

Jack Irelan, the school's attorney, asked Mr. Korngold to read him parts of the warrant. Mr. Korngold did and then listened for a long time. He sat down on his chair. His secretary had come into the office. She stood watching with both hands pressed over her mouth. "But that's impossible," said Mr. Korngold. "Not this kid, Jack. It's impossible . . . It's . . . Okay, Jack . . . Okay, Jack . . . Okay, call me back as soon as . . . Okay." He hung up the phone.

"What is it, Bernie?" said the secretary.

Mr. Korngold looked up into her face. "Lynda," he said, "my God. Jack thinks they've arrested him for . . . for some terror-related thing . . . for . . . terrorism."

Mr. Korngold called Jennifer, but she already knew. Four men had shown up at her apartment, had presented their badges and a search warrant. They had pushed their way past her, and, when she rushed to stop them, two of the men restrained her while the other men went into Zaharia's room. They went through all his belongings. They took some things, including a small notebook and a diary.

"They didn't arrest Jenny," said Michael.

"Where is she now?" said Louis.

"With me," said Michael.

"Good," said Louis. "Is she all right?"

"Not really," said Michael.

* * *

"Peter Sanchez speaking."

"Mr. Sanchez, this is Louis Morgon."

"Mr. Morgon. Nice to hear from you. Have you changed your mind?"

"Mr. Sanchez, the FBI has just arrested a boy named Zaharia Lefort, an Algerian who is a student at the Potomac School."

"Zaharia . . . ?"

"Zaharia Lefort."

"L-e-f-o r-t? First name, Z-a-h-a-r-i-a?"

"That's right." Louis could hear the keys of a computer clicking.

"I'm sorry, but I don't know why you're asking about this." Louis heard the computer keys again. Louis waited. "Oh, I see," said Sanchez. His voice had gone cold.

"I'm ready to undertake the project you approached me about," said Louis.

"That plan is no longer operative, Mr. Morgon."

"Really? That's odd," said Louis.

"I'm sorry, Mr. Morgon . . ."

"Mr. Sanchez, the project is still very much 'operative' on this end. In fact, you could say it's in go-ahead mode."

"Mr. Morgon . . ."

"With or without you, Mr. Sanchez. I'd prefer it were with you, but I'm perfectly prepared to proceed without you. I have a ticket to Cairo, where, as you know, I'll try to make contact with Abu Massad, among others. That ticket is for one week from today. If you intend to run my operation, I suggest you come back to France before then. Let's meet in Paris this time, shall we?" Louis hung up the phone. When it rang, he let it ring. Then he called Pauline. "I'm coming to Paris," he said. "I need your help."

Peter Sanchez arrived in Paris the following morning. When he called Louis's number, the call was forwarded to a cell phone. Louis answered. The two men arranged to meet that afternoon on a bench in the Jardin du Luxembourg.

"See? That's him down there," said Louis. They were watching from Pauline's window.

"He's early," said Pauline.

"He's getting the lay of the land. And he knows I'm watching from somewhere. He wants me to feel reassured."

"What an insane business you were in," she said. "And do you?"

"Do I what?"

"Feel reassured."

"Just watch us," said Louis. "If I stand up before he does, call the police and tell them there's an emergency in the park. . . . Say there's an assault going on."

Pauline stood at the window and watched. After some time, she saw Louis emerge from the trees. He crossed a broad gravel expanse toward Sanchez.

The leaves of the plane trees had fallen and were blowing about making scraping noises against the gravel. Sanchez stood up as Louis approached.

"Mr. Sanchez," said Louis.

"I had no idea," said Sanchez. "There's no reason for you to believe me. But I had no idea."

"Tell me what happened," said Louis, and sat down beside him.

"Phillip Dimitrius, the man who was following you in Algiers," said Sanchez. "And the Agency computers. A great deal of information—like your files for example—goes into the computers and is forgotten. We've got so much raw data coming in, there is no way it could ever be analyzed. It stays there, forgotten, in huge computer archives. That is, until a search for a phrase or a name or a case number brings something to the surface. In that moment something dead and forgotten instantly becomes alive and dangerous. It's not supposed to happen, and usually it doesn't. Everything is compartmentalized and firewalled to prevent something like this from happening.

"There were files on you, of course, including a false biography marking you as a traitor and a terrorist. You know all about that. Anyway, those files were safe. Whoever cleaned up the mess made certain they would not be available, except with a special access code. But they left the name of the files—Louis Morgon/France—available for anyone with Agency access to see."

"Why were those files even kept?" said Louis.

"I don't know," said Sanchez. "They should have been expunged. You're wondering whether anyone wanted to hang on to them, just in case. I don't know that either. But I doubt it. I think it was probably the sheer mass of information. There's not time to expunge everything that should be expunged. I'm looking into it. Before Dimitrius happened on them, they had not been accessed since they were active— four years ago.

"Anyway, Phillip Dimitrius is part of a terrorist task force focusing on France. He is known as a persistent and dogged researcher. He trolls Agency files, looking for suggestive leads. That is how your name eventually popped up on his screen. Having the file locked up made it especially tantalizing to him."

"Suggestive leads," said Louis.

"Yes," said Peter. "Suggestive leads."

Phillip Dimitrius had spent weeks staring at his computer screen in a small cubicle in the South Annex at Langley headquarters. He sat with his face close to the screen and his pen poised over a yellow pad.

As a boy Phillip had spoken a few lines in a school play. There is no accounting for why that brief experience affected him in the momentous way it did. But, from that moment forward, drama became the constant paradigm of his understanding. He saw everything in dramatic terms: his courtship and marriage, the deaths of his parents, the births of Phillip Junior, then Samantha, then David. And in his mind all these vivid and homely scenes of his domestic drama laid the groundwork for the larger drama, the gripping action playing itself out on the great world stage.

Phillip's role in the greater drama was, he readily admitted, a minor one. But he was determined it would not remain an insignificant one. He believed himself to be a catalyst for resolution in the epic struggle between good and evil. That was how he found and locked on to Louis Morgon's name and decided to follow wherever it led—to France and back to Washington. To Algiers and to Cairo. It suited the great drama so perfectly that Phillip could not imagine it was a drama of his own construction.

As Peter Sanchez explained it, "The more Dimitrius looked around, the better it got. He found Samad al Nhouri, who had been your contact in the sixties. He found Moamar al Nhouri, who had been active in anti-American and national-liberation organizations. He found Camille Lefort, Sabiha Falool, and Zaharia Lefort. They all had interesting connections with Louis Morgon, who, as far as Dimitrius could determine, had been abrubtly dismissed from the Agency for serious infractions—maybe crimes—and now was, possibly, a terrorist.

"Zaharia Lefort also had a file. He had been in trouble with the police in France and had been on the run until he was sent back to Algiers."

"He was fourteen. The police killed his father. He was fleeing for his life."

"All that may be true, but the file didn't give the exonerating details. Anyway, Zaharia Lefort had been involved with you. That was what attracted Dimitrius. And Zaharia was all grown up now. He had applied for a visa to go to school in the United States. You can see how it added up in his mind.

"By now Dimitrius had sent a report up the line. When Zaharia Lefort showed up in Washington—on a student visa, with a one-way ticket, not long after meeting with you in Algiers—someone decided to bring him in. I don't know who made the decision, or why, but it shouldn't have happened. None of it should have happened."

Louis studied Peter Sanchez's face. "That is everything I know up to now," said Peter. "I beg you not to go to Egypt. It will only make matters worse. For Zaharia Lefort. And for you."

"Where is the boy?" said Louis.

Sanchez looked away. He folded and unfolded his hands.

"Where is he?" said Louis.

"A lot of foreigners they pick up on terror charges these days are sent—renditioned—somewhere else," said Peter Sanchez. "It's the way this administration avoids dealing with the courts."

"Guantanamo?" said Louis.

"Tajikistan or Uzbekistan, I think."

"Which one?" said Louis. "Where?"

"I'm still trying to find out. I'll let you know the minute I do. What a colossal fuckup."

Back in Pauline's apartment Louis sat with his head in his

hands. "I was going to stand up when he said that," said Louis. "'A colossal fuckup.' I wanted the police to come and arrest the son of a bitch. To arrest both of us."

"So they didn't take the boy to force you . . . ?" said Pauline.

"I don't know," said Louis. "I think his story is close to true, except I don't know where Sanchez fits into his own story. What's his part in all of this? Is Dimitrius working for him? Did Sanchez order the arrest himself? I just don't know."

"So you're not going to Egypt?" said Pauline.

"I told Sanchez I wasn't going," said Louis.

"What did he say?" said Pauline.

"'Thank you.' He said, 'Thank you.'"

"So you're not going?"

"I'm going."

"Why?"

Louis hesitated. He studied Pauline.

"Tell me what you're thinking, Louis."

"You didn't ask for this, Pauline. It's not fair to you. Everyone I come close to is in danger. I am poison."

"Stop feeling sorry for yourself," she said. That was exactly what Solesme would have said. "Tell me what you're thinking."

"When they send people to these foreign prisons, it's to avoid due process. They can hold them as long as they like. And they do what they want with them. They can use extreme measures—torture—to extract information. Even people who are known to be innocent don't come back easily. There have been a few cases in the newspapers . . ."

"I've read about them," said Pauline.

"There was a German recently," said Louis.

"I remember," said Pauline.

"They snatched him on a business trip. His family knew nothing about what had happened to him. He was in prison for months. His only crime was having a Turkish name. Then they turn them loose on their own schedule. If they turn them loose at all. No one can help them. No lawyers, no hearings, nothing."

"So why are you going to Cairo?"

"To look for something to trade for Zaharia, something to force them to release him. My God, Pauline"—tears welled up in Louis's eyes—"he's just a boy."

She held his head in her arms.

V

Zaharia wore an orange jumpsuit. He was in shackles and leg irons. He kept his eyes wide open, even though he was blindfolded. He stared straight ahead hoping that some idea of what was happening would emerge somehow from the blackness before him.

He could hear other prisoners' voices above the noise of the plane's engines. They were fearful or angry or pleading. Their questions—in English, Arabic, other languages—went unanswered. Sometimes someone would start wailing.

The guards were not brutal. They spoke softly, and only when necessary. He could not tell how many prisoners there were. Or how many guards. He knew there was a guard seated beside him. When Zaharia had to go to the bathroom, the guard took his arm and helped him out of his seat. The guard walked him to the bathroom. Zaharia shuffled along because of the leg irons. "The blindfold stays on," said the guard. "Piss sitting down. Like a girl." He held the door open and watched until Zaharia was finished.

They had given him an injection in the beginning because he had become hysterical. He had remembered the sight of the policemen killing his father. He remembered watching them through the keyhole. So, for the first hours of his detention, he slept. Then he sat still, or rocked in place. Then he was taken in a bus and put on the airplane.

Zaharia did not know which direction they were flying. He did not know whether it was night or day. The trip went on and on. He had no sense of how long it lasted. The droning engine put him to sleep. Then he would wake up and have to figure out what was happening to him all over again.

The plane landed. After a while it took off again. When it landed again, they were escorted off the plane and onto buses. They rolled over bumpy roads for a long time before they stopped. Zaharia could hear that there was more than one bus unloading. By now no one was crying or asking desperate questions.

The prisoners were led into a building and down some stairs. Zaharia was put into a cell by himself. He was blinded by the light when his blindfold was removed. The guard turned and slammed the iron door behind him. Zaharia heard other cell doors slamming as other prisoners were put in cells.

His cell was three meters by three meters. It was lit by a single bulb in a metal cage attached to the ceiling. The concrete walls were damp. There was a metal bunk with a straw-filled mattress. There was a slop bucket. Some of the other cells had toilets. A slop bucket was better, since you emptied and rinsed it every day. The toilets were filthy and often didn't work.

Zaharia had just sat down on the bed when the door opened and two men came in. They wore camouflage pants and shirts, but they were unshaved and didn't look like soldiers. "Take off clothes," said one. Zaharia didn't understand at first; the man had a strange accent. "Take off clothes!" he said again. "I am doctor. I give examination."

"Everything?" said Zaharia.

"Take off all clothes," said the doctor. "I give examination."

Zaharia stood naked in front of the two men. The doctor had a flashlight and a stick. "Open mouth. Put head back." He shined the flashlight into Zaharia's mouth. He used the stick to push his cheeks to the side and lift his tongue. "Lift arms," he said. He jammed the stick under Zaharia's arms.

"Lift cock," he said. He pointed with the flashlight. He turned it on and looked. "Lift balls," he said and shined the light again. He went around behind Zaharia. "Bend over and spread." Zaharia did as he was told. He felt the stick circling the edge of his anus.

"Stand up," said the doctor. "Finished. Good healthy," he said.

After many more hours another guard came in with a metal bowl of stew. Zaharia ate everything. Then he used his finger to get the parts his spoon would not reach.

Zaharia could not tell when it was day or when it was night. There were no windows, and the light was always on. The mattress was damp and smelled strongly of disinfectant. He slept anyway. All he knew was, when he woke up, it was later than when he had gone to sleep. Some time had passed, and he was that much closer to this being over. There were noises in the corridor, people coming and going, murmured words. But that was all.

Zaharia heard a tapping on the wall. Five taps, then six taps, then seven, all the way to twenty-six. Then the taps started over with one, then two. Zaharia tapped out his name. It took a long time to tap out a Z. He was glad his name had three As. The man next door was named Ahmed. He said he was a medical student from Jordan. *Don't give up hope,* he tapped. *Praise Allah.* One day he tapped out, *Learn to hold breath.* Another day he tapped, *Act like drowning.* Then one day his tapping went silent. Zaharia tapped, *Ahmed are you there.* There was no answer. He tapped again later. There was no answer.

Two guards came to Zaharia's cell. They blindfolded him and led him down the long corridor. They took him down some stairs and into a room. They removed his blindfold. He stood in front of a table facing a seated man. There were two other men standing behind the man. They all wore camouflage pants and shirts. The seated man was reading a sheet of paper. He looked up. He smiled. "Hello, Zaharia."

Zaharia said hello.

"Do you know why you are here?" said the man.

"No," said Zaharia.

"How old are you, Zaharia?"

"Almost seventeen."

"When is your birthday?"

"December 6."

"Soon," said the man. His face got sad. "You're so young, Zaharia. Your whole life is ahead of you. And yet, here you are, already mixed up in such a terrible business."

"What terrible business?"

"Oh, Zaharia, I think you know what I'm talking about. You're much too young to feel such hate. Why do you hate America?"

"I don't hate America. I am a student. I came to America to go to school."

"Does the name"—he mentioned a name—"mean anything to you?"

"No," said Zaharia.

"What about . . . ?" He mentioned another name. Again Zaharia said no.

"What about Louis Morgon?" said the man.

"Yes. Louis Morgon is my friend," said Zaharia.

"Louis Morgon, the terrorist, is your friend? Well, that is

exactly what I mean. You can see, can't you, son? Your so-called friend has gotten you in a lot of trouble. You maybe should have chosen your friends more carefully."

Interrogation is an art more than it is a science. An unskilled interrogator might phrase something in a particular way, intending to soften up his subject. And yet his phrasing might have exactly the opposite effect. Zaharia's interrogator was from Texas, where calling someone son is a sign of affection and intimacy. And that was how he meant it. He wanted to disarm the boy, to show him that he cared about him and had his best interest at heart. The effect on Zaharia, however, was like a slap in the face.

Louis would have advised Zaharia to tell the man anything he wanted to know. Tell him that Louis was a terrorist and that he knew where Louis's bomb-making factory was. It doesn't matter, Louis would have said. They just need some words to put in their logs. They don't really know, or care, whether they are true or not. And they might just treat you better if you talk.

Instead, by the time the interrogator had called Zaharia son twice more, Zaharia had resolved not to answer any questions at all. When it became clear that Zaharia was not going to cooperate, he was turned over to the two guards, who forced him to his knees and pushed his head into the toilet. They held him there ten, fifteen, twenty seconds, finally pulling him up, gasping and crying. "Louis Morgon is my friend," he cried. "Why are you doing this?"

"Do you have any other friends?"

"Yes, of course," he said. "Jennifer, Michael, Arnold Chan, I have lots of friends."

Before he could take a breath, his head was back in the water. After the next dunking, he was brought up vomiting. He staggered back to his cell, held up by the two guards, where he vomited some more.

Zaharia remembered the messages Ahmed had tapped on his wall. *Learn to hold breath. Act like drowning.* He practiced taking in air quickly and holding his breath for as long as he could. He timed himself using his heartbeat. The next time they dunked him, he fought them a reasonable length of time, went limp, and was brought up gasping. He even retched convincingly.

Later, when they brought him back for another interrogation, there was a car battery on the table. One of the guards was attaching wires to the battery. "Do you know what this is, son?" said the man from Texas, holding the loose ends of the wire in front of Zaharia's face. "It's electricity. My colleagues here are going to see how good you are at acting like you're being electrocuted." The man from Texas left the room. This time Zaharia had to be carried back to his cell when the treatment was finished. No questions had even been asked.

The abuse came and went. Like bad weather. Days would pass without Zaharia being taken from his cell. Then the guards would suddenly appear. He would be taken to the interrogation room. He would be made to stand up until his legs collapsed. He was young and strong, so this could take a very long time. He was carried back to his cell.

One day a doctor—a real doctor—came to his cell to examine him. The doctor, an American, asked Zaharia his name and where he was from. He listened to his chest through a stethoscope. He thumped on his back and tapped his knee with a little hammer. He lifted his eyelids and peered into his eyes with a bright light. He moved his finger back and forth in front of Zaharia's face and told him to follow the motion with his eyes. Zaharia did not have any wounds. He was not sick or malnourished or suffering any other physical deficits.

"Please, Doctor," he whispered, "help me. I am being tortured."

"No you're not," said the doctor. Zaharia's interrogation was allowed to continue.

VI

As the plane descended, Louis peered out across the great river delta. Cairo sprawled across the landscape and into the distant, shimmering haze. Buildings covered both banks of the Nile and the islands too. The city reached far into the desert. Skyscrapers poked into the sky where previously there had been only minarets.

Uniformed policemen studied Louis's passport and riffled through his bag. He found his way through the crowded terminal to the street, where he waited in line for a taxi. Had the cabs always been black and white? Louis could not remember.

They drove along grand boulevards past government palaces and public gardens that made Louis think of Paris. The cab turned past the guardian lions onto Qasr el Nil Bridge. They passed the opera house, crossed another bridge—Louis could not remember the name—to the east bank, and stopped just past the Egyptian Museum. *"Voila,"* said the driver. He took Louis for French. "Toledo Hotel, mister," he said. Louis paid him. The cab drove off. Louis carried his bag inside.

The telephone rang in Renard's office. "Mr. Renard," said Peter Sanchez in serviceable French, "my name is Peter Sanchez."

Renard sat up straight in his chair. "Who?" he said, managing to sound indifferent.

"Peter Sanchez. I'm sure Louis Morgon mentioned me to you. I'm trying to reach Louis, but he isn't answering his telephone."

"How can I help you, Mr. Sanchez?" said Renard. He stepped to the window. There were no unfamiliar cars parked on the square.

"I don't suppose you would know where I can find Mr. Morgon."

"I think he's in Paris."

"Paris," said Peter.

"Visiting a friend," said Renard.

"Visiting a friend," said Peter.

Stop repeating everything I say, Renard said to himself.

"Would that by any chance be Pauline Vasiltschenko?"

"May I ask why you're asking all these questions, Mr. . . . ?"

"Peter Sanchez. As I said, Mr. Renard, I'm trying to find Louis Morgon."

"Oh, yes. He thought you might call," Renard said. "He asked me to take a message."

"A message." Peter Sanchez was thinking. "No," he said finally. "No, thank you." Then: "If you see Louis, please ask him to call me." He hung up before Renard could respond. Renard wondered whether he might have played it too dumb.

When Peter Sanchez called Pauline, he got a similar response. "He's not here. He's out right now," said Pauline. When Peter called back later, she said, "He was here for dinner, but now he's out again. At a concert. I don't know which one."

"Perfect," said Louis when Pauline reported the conversation. "Thank you."

"Explain your thinking," she said.

"I want him to think I've gone to Cairo. And I want him to think that I don't *want* him to think I've gone."

Pauline thought about that for a moment. "The charade seems pretty complicated, Louis. And pretty transparent. Do you also want him to think you're not very clever?" said Pauline.

"That would be helpful," said Louis. "It adds one more layer to the confusion."

"Confusion is a good thing?" She was trying to take it all in.

"We don't have much else on our side," said Louis. "Not yet."

Pauline was pleased that he had said we. "And how is it there?"

"I don't recognize the place," said Louis. "It's fast and modern and cosmopolitan. I haven't found the charming and mysterious old Cairo yet."

"I love Cairo," said Pauline. "What are you going to do now?"

"I'm going to wait for Sanchez to show up. Meanwhile, I'll see if I can stir things up. Jam a stick into the hornets' nest."

Louis's room was on the fifth floor of the Toledo, which was the top floor. He opened the shutters, and a soft, hot breeze enveloped him. He hung his clothes in the wooden armoire and put his bag in the closet.

Cairo had several spy hotels, but the Toledo was not one of them. The one usually frequented by Americans and Brits was the Ramses, just off Ramses Square. The Ramses was a belle époch palace of golden sandstone. There was a statue of the pharaoh Ramses out front in the center of the circular drive.

As usual in such places, the lobby of the Ramses was a sort of clandestine marketplace, with people—both men and women these days—trading stories and waiting for some useful tidbit to come their way. Intelligence work is, as it has always been, a peculiar mix of closely guarded secrets and wild gossip, and very often it is impossible to tell which is which. A few ordinary tourists came and went, giving the place an air of normalcy.

Louis walked up to four American men standing near the front desk. They had drinks in their hands. They stopped talking as Louis approached. They waited expectantly, hopefully even. After all, when someone of Louis's disheveled mien—he wore battered walking shoes, his seersucker jacket was rumpled, his white hair drifted like a cloud about his head—approached in that determined way, you had the distinct impression that he was in possession of information he could hardly wait to share. All you had to do was coax him a bit, and something useful would come spilling out.

"I'm looking for Sanchez," said Louis. "Peter Sanchez. Has anyone seen him?" He smiled and peered at the men through glasses that made his eyes look huge.

This was what Louis called his arrow-in-the-air strategy. He waited while it fell to earth. In fact, one of the men—the oldest of the four—looked around as though an arrow might actually have struck the floor somewhere behind him.

"Who?" said one of the others.

"I don't see him," said the man who had turned around to look.

"When you see him . . ." Louis seemed to think things over. "Oh, never mind," he said, and wandered off.

"Who is Peter Sanchez?" said the youngest man in the group.

"You don't know Peter Sanchez?" said the oldest man.

One of the other men caught on and echoed the oldest man's astonishment. "You don't know Peter Sanchez?"

"No," said the youngest man, feeling more and more as though he had just given something away he shouldn't have.

The oldest man took pity on him. "Peter Sanchez? How the hell should I know?" he said. The others guffawed, including the youngest, relieved that it was all a joke. "And who the hell was *that?*"

The four watched Louis walk up to a man and a woman across the room and ask them whether *they* had seen Peter. Before the afternoon was out, Louis had confronted thirty or forty people in the lobby, in the bar, in the newsstand, inquiring about Peter Sanchez. They would all remember Louis, and they would remember the name Peter Sanchez. In fact Peter Sanchez became the punch line in the Ramses's best joke of the week.

Louis figured that, if Peter Sanchez chased him to Cairo, and it was reasonable to assume that he would, then Peter would probably begin his search at one of the spy hotels. The Ramses was the most likely one. Peter arrived the following afternoon. He was in the lounge having a drink, when he could have sworn he heard his name spoken by someone standing at the bar. He walked up to the bar just in time to hear the words "Who the hell is Peter Sanchez?" followed by gales of laughter.

Peter went to the concierge desk and asked whether anyone

had left any messages for him. The concierge checked in the small drawer in front of him and handed Peter an envelope addressed in overlarge letters:

Mr. Peter Sanchez
Central Intelligence Agency

"Jesus Christ, Louis," he muttered. Then he had to laugh.

Dear Mister Sanchez,
Thank you for coming to Cairo. I would like to meet with you, to get as much up-to-date information as possible about the people I am going to meet. I will be in the breakfast room of the Hotel Ramses at 9 o'clock tomorrow morning.
Louis Morgon

By nine o'clock, the breakfast room was mostly empty of guests. The French doors had been opened onto the sun porch, and the service people were clearing the tables. Louis sat facing out into the gardens, which were lush with oleander and hibiscus and lilies and papyrus and date palms. A fountain sent a jet of water into the air. It splashed into the scalloped basin, its spray causing miniature rainbows to form and quickly dissipate. White lotus blossoms swayed gently. They glowed as though they were lit from within.

"Mr. Morgon," said Peter.

"Please sit down," said Louis without taking his eyes off the garden. He sipped from a glass of tea.

Peter sat down. He waved away the waiter. "You're playing a dangerous game," said Peter.

"Here's what I need from you," said Louis. "I need likely addresses, profiles, history, everything you've got for the names you've given me."

"You're out of your mind," said Peter.

"Maybe," said Louis. "Again: I need addresses, history on all the names. From Abu Massad on down. As soon as we've done that, I'll start making contact and exploring possible channels up the line. We'll have to wait and see where it takes me. But I'm starting right away.

"I also need something to trade with. Some outdated, but viable, secrets. Iranian missile sites. That sort of thing. And I need you to be my spotter, my backup, to keep me in sight while all this is going on. I don't know how much you know about this part of the world, but you're going to have to learn fast."

"You know, " said Peter, "there's very little likelihood that you'll succeed at any of this."

"That *we'll* succeed," said Louis. "There's little likelihood that *we'll* succeed. I quite agree. But you better do everything in your power to see that we do. For your own sake, and for the sake of those you care about. You're here on your own, aren't you? You're freelancing."

Peter did not answer.

"I thought so. What's more, you're running an unauthorized operation with me, a thoroughly discredited operative . . ."

"You made sure it's unauthorized," said Peter.

"That's right, I did," said Louis. "And I also made sure half the guests in this hotel know you're here. You're way out of bounds, as far as the Agency is concerned. So, if you don't go home with a big payoff, then you might as well not go home at all.

"They'll destroy your career, you know," said Louis. "If you're lucky. If you're not, they'll go after you personally. They demand success. And the only thing that will satisfy them, if we don't succeed, will be your eternal unhappiness. They call it discipline. Or correction. But it comes down to revenge. People who can send seventeen-year-olds to prisons in Uzbekistan will do pretty much anything. You've read my file. Now you're going to see for yourself what it's like."

Peter and Louis looked at one another for a long minute. Finally Peter stood up. "Come with me," he said. He led the way upstairs to his room. He turned on his computer and opened his files. Louis took out his pocket notebook and wrote.

The first link in the chain of informers was a man named Giorgio Smarth. He had tried other aliases over the years but then stayed with Giorgio Smarth. He had first turned up during Vietnam with dubious information and contacts for sale. Louis had first known him in Cairo. He had met him again in

Beirut and in Washington and finally back in Cairo. Smarth said he was American, but he wasn't. No one knew what he was.

Smarth called himself a "currency trader," which meant he was in the smuggling business—money, drugs, weapons, chemicals. But Smarth's most lucrative commodity had always been information. It was easier to handle and easier to dispose of than material commodities. Smarth sold information for money. After all, he needed to live. But he always preferred that there be a swap involved as well—one tidbit for another. It was a kind of insurance against betrayal by the other party.

Besides, Smarth had an impeccable ear for valuable information. He always seemed to know from whom a particular piece of information might fetch him something even better. Smarth operated from several cafés located on the edges of various bazaars. He found safety and comfort among the crowds.

Louis found him at a market café on the west bank of the Nile. Boats bobbed in the sunlight behind the market stalls. People milled about. Women eyed the vegetables and fruits suspiciously, turning them over, squeezing them despite the vendors' protestations. They bent over the crates of salted and dried fish, sniffing them, looking into their dead eyes. The air was filled with the noise of vendors crying their wares, customers haggling, men arguing about football, and, in the background, the relentless traffic.

Smarth's eyes narrowed as Louis approached. He looked away quickly.

"Hello, Giorgio," said Louis.

Smarth sipped his coffee and pretended not to hear.

"It's Louis Coburn," said Louis. Giorgio's eyes snapped to attention. They narrowed and then widened.

"Louis," said Giorgio. He stared in astonishment. He looked around, as if to see what other ghosts might suddenly emerge unexpectedly from out of his past. "My God, Coburn." He did not stand or offer his hand. "Sit down. Tea, right?" Giorgio turned and signaled to the waiter. "Tea," he shouted. "Cardamom. Am I right?"

"You're right," said Louis. "And you, still coffee with too much sugar?"

Giorgio laughed as though Louis had made the funniest joke in the world. Giorgio's teeth were mostly gone. His laughter ended in a fit of coughing.

"How's business?" said Louis when the coughing finally subsided.

Giorgio peered intently into his handkerchief, then gave his mouth one more wipe. "Cairo is changed," said Giorgio. "Business? What business? I barely stay alive. And you, Coburn? I can't believe *you're* still at it."

"Only on special occasions," said Louis.

"Aha," said Giorgio. He took a sip of coffee. "Special occasions. So, what is the special occasion?"

Louis smiled. "You never used to be so direct, Giorgio."

Giorgio shrugged. A beggar approached their table, and Giorgio shooed her away. "You see? There's still the old Cairo. No. No. I'm old, that's all. And sick. I just don't enjoy the game anymore. You tell me what you've got and what you want. If I like what you've got, and I've got what you want, then we deal. That's how I work these days. I can't do the old song and dance anymore." He laughed and pointed to where his leg used to be. "There are no one-legged dancers. Diabetes," he said.

"I'm looking for some people." Louis mentioned some names. Giorgio shrugged. "Don't know them."

"What about Abu Massad?" said Louis.

"That crazy bastard? Him I know and wish I didn't."

"I need to find him."

"No you don't, Louis. Believe me, you don't. He's a crazy fucking Taliban."

"Is he still in Cairo?"

"Don't ask me things you already know," said Giorgio. "Of course he is."

"How do I get to him?"

"He's surrounded by thugs," said Giorgio. "No, no. I can't help you there. They'd come after me."

"They'd never know it came from you," said Louis. "Besides, I've got something for you."

Giorgio snorted. "Don't be ridiculous. Anyway, it's not worth it."

"You don't know what I'm offering," said Louis.

"Don't tell me, I can't do it. I don't want to know. I can't do it."

Louis leaned over and whispered in Giorgio's ear.

Giorgio sat bolt upright. "Are you crazy? Are you trying to get me killed? What the hell can I do with that kind of information? Jesus, Coburn."

"It's worth a lot," said Louis. "Iranian nuclear sites. Test results. The Saudis would love to get it. The Israelis. Anybody would. You'll have the files tomorrow."

"No, no. I can't do it."

"And a small down payment today. Five hundred."

"A thousand," said Giorgio. "And files and photos tomorrow."

"A thousand dollars?" said Louis.

"Euros," said Giorgio with a thin smile. Louis gave him a thousand euros.

"One of Abu Massad's killers is a client of mine," said Giorgio. "He can get you into his inner sanctum. But that is all he can do," he said. "He can't get you out."

VII

Louis took a taxi to a particular street corner. After several minutes, a man walked up, took his arm, and steered him into a narrow alley. At the other end of the alley a Land Cruiser was waiting, along with three armed men. They tied his hands and blindfolded him.

Louis sat in the backseat between two of the men. He tried to listen for distinctive sounds as they drove, but the windows of the Land Cruiser were up, and rap music was playing. He could hear Cairo's chaotic traffic, but that was no help. They drove for about an hour. The traffic noises disappeared. The ride become rougher. The Land Cruiser lurched and swayed over the damaged road.

Finally they slowed. One of the men jumped out. They

drove into a garage. The car doors opened, and the other men got out. Someone took Louis's arm and helped him from the car. They led him through a door. "Sit," said one of the men. Louis sat down on a straight-backed wooden chair. They left him alone. The only sound was the buzzing of a lamp somewhere above him.

A door opened and someone entered the room. He lifted Louis's arm and Louis stood. The man steered him across the room. He opened a door. They walked down a narrow hallway. Louis kept bumping into the wall. Again Louis was told to sit. The blindfold was removed.

Abu Massad was seated at a writing table in front of him. He was thin and pale. His folded hands trembled slightly. Behind him a small window looked out on an enclosed courtyard. Abu Massad lifted himself from his chair with difficulty and, leaning on the writing table for support, peered hard at Louis. He said in a high, reedy voice, "I remember you. Louis Coburn. You are not someone I expected to see again in this lifetime." He sat back down.

"I am grateful," said Louis, "that you agreed to see me, Abu Massad." He bowed his head toward the old man.

Abu Massad frowned and lowered his eyes. "Let us have some tea," he said to the man who had escorted Louis into the room. The man left the room and returned with a lacquer tray bearing a teapot and two small bowls. Abu Massad instructed the young man to untie Louis's hands. Then he sent the man out of the room. Louis and Abu Massad drank tea in silence.

Finally Abu Massad spoke. "I do not welcome strangers. Tell me why you have come."

"Abu Massad," said Louis, "a great deal has changed since we last met."

"A great deal," said Abu Massad. "The world has changed. And I have changed with it. I have put aside foolish dreams."

"Which foolish dreams?" said Louis.

"A young man's foolish dreams. Dreams you helped foster in me. I do not like to think back on that time. Foolish dreams of peace and democracy in Egypt. Ridiculous. It was a time of wandering in the desert for me." Abu Massad paused. "It agitates me to think about it, even after all this time. The path to righteousness leads only through the Holy Koran." The cup began shaking in his hand, and he set it down. "What do I have to do with your ways any longer? Nothing. Nothing. Why have you come to bother me? I am old. I do not welcome this agitation. I have found the path to righteousness."

Louis said nothing.

"I know that look," said Abu Massad.

"Forgive me, Abu Massad. There are too many paths to righteousness for me to know which is the correct one."

"There is but one path. Why do you contradict me in my own home? What do you want?"

"I want to find my way to Osama bin Laden."

"Of course you do. Everyone does. I am not surprised. And your CIA masters think that I can help you get to him."

"They do," said Louis.

"Then they are not only misguided," said Abu Massad, "they are fools."

"I am not surprised to hear you say that," said Louis. "And I agree with you. You see, I too have learned something with time. They are fools."

Abu Massad stroked his pointed gray beard and studied Louis. "Let me teach you something else, Louis Coburn. You can take it back to your American masters, although I think it is too late for them. You Americans are always too late. You are always searching for what is finished, while the next thing has already begun.

"First of all, bin Laden is probably dead, buried under some mountain in Pakistan. The videotapes and sound recordings that al Qaeda releases from time to time are either old or they are forgeries."

"How do you know this to be true?" said Louis.

Abu Massad ignored him. "Secondly, even if he is alive, what does he possibly matter? His time is past. If you kill him, you will only turn a ridiculous man in a painted beard into a martyr. Anyway, he would flee before me or anyone I sent. In me he sees Allah's avenging angel." Abu Massad was on his feet now. "I charge bin Laden with using God's Holy Word, the Holy Koran, to advance his own corrupt political dreams."

"And your dreams?" said Louis.

Abu Massad was unsteady on his feet. "Do not interrupt me." He swayed to and fro in the grip of his passion. His eyes were wide and watery. His hands were planted on the table for support. "You dare compare my dreams with bin Laden's? My dreams," he said, "are as the Holy Prophet's dreams. I dream of a time when all worldly law and power springs from the Prophet's Holy Word. I want to transform Egypt into a Muslim Holy Land, to restore the greatness and power that was once ours. And to send Osama bin Laden and his fellow infidels straight to hell."

"Then why not make me the instrument of your dreams?" said Louis. "Make our common purpose—the destruction of this man—work for you."

Abu Massad sat down. He leaned forward in his chair. He reached for the teapot and filled the two bowls. The aroma of spiced tea once again filled the room. He gave Louis a hard look. "You begin to interest me, Louis Coburn."

"I am glad to hear it," said Louis.

"Except I cannot help you find him."

"Because he is dead," said Louis, smiling slightly.

"There is that, of course," said Abu Massad. "And there is the act of treachery. Whatever my desires, sending you to him would entail the greatest act of treachery imaginable. Even my own followers would see it that way. Think of it. Waging Holy War against bin Laden is one thing. But sending the infidel to destroy him would be treachery and cowardice and . . . it is too much to contemplate. My life would be finished." He lifted his bowl in both hands and took a sip.

"Anyway," he continued, "you Americans are simpletons. Bin Laden does not even matter anymore."

"I do not need him to matter," said Louis. "As long as those I work for think he matters."

"Who are you working for, Louis Coburn?"

"The CIA."

"Of course. But who else?"

Louis thought for a moment. "A boy," he said. "An Algerian schoolboy. An innocent. Taken prisoner by the American FBI."

"One of many." Abu Massad waved his hand.

"He is a friend of mine," said Louis.

"I think I am beginning to understand."

"Perhaps you are."

"You are looking for . . . leverage against . . . his captors."

"Something like that."

"You are too late to get bin Laden, you know."

"Because he is dead."

Abu Massad did not smile. "Because his eggs have hatched and his offspring have flown to the four corners of the world. Oh, you can look in Waziristan, in Afghanistan, in Indonesia. But it is too late for that. The people you'll find there are servants, lackeys, peons. If you want to find the terror brains now, look where they can do the most harm, and where they can most easily disappear, where there is the kind of anonymity they need."

"Where would that be?" said Louis.

"Look closer to home."

"Closer to home?"

"Copenhagen, Berlin, Madrid, New York. In fact, I went to Paris last year," said Abu Massad. "I stayed in Clichy-sous-Bois. Do you know it? That part of Paris has miles of high-rise slums filled with undocumented, anonymous people. These people, millions of them, are prisoners of their own dire circumstances.

"When the police go there, they brutalize the people. But mostly they do not go there, because if they did, it might all explode again. The government, which ignores their plight, leaves them alone for the same reason. They are, as Sarkozy said, scum. The only freedom they have is the freedom to destroy. You can find the same situation in a hundred cities. If I were you, I would look close to home. Look in Paris."

"Give me a name," said Louis.

And to his surprise Abu Massad did. "Fareed Terzani," he said.

In the backseat of the Land Cruiser once again, blindfolded, his hands bound, Louis could tell they were not driving toward Cairo. There was no traffic to be heard, except for an occasional truck roaring past. When they stopped finally, and Louis's blindfold was removed, it was night. The only light came from the distant horizon. They all got out and stood in the headlights of the Land Cruiser.

"Kneel," said one of the men. When Louis didn't move

quickly enough, they pushed him to the ground. Instead of shooting him though, they got in the Land Cruiser and drove off.

Louis was still working to untie his hands when Peter Sanchez walked up. He helped Louis to his feet and removed the ropes from his wrists.

"They only meant to scare me," said Louis, brushing the dust from his pants. "It was a message. 'Don't come back.'"

"Maybe," said Peter Sanchez.

"Were you behind us the entire time?"

"I followed you from the moment they picked you up," said Peter Sanchez.

"Did they see you?"

"Only at the end," said Peter Sanchez. "When I flashed my headlights."

"Ah," said Louis.

They got in Peter's car. Peter turned around and drove toward the lights glowing faintly on the horizon. "What did you get?" said Peter.

"A lecture. Otherwise, nothing."

"Nothing?" Peter looked over at Louis.

He saw an old man. Louis was slumped on the seat, his hands forgotten on his lap, his entire body slack, his hair disheveled, even for Louis. "Nothing," he said.

"Are you all right?" said Peter.

"I'm going home," said Louis.

"Home?! You're going home?! You brought me all the

way here just so you could go home? Just like that?" said Peter.

"Not just like that. I have cancer."

"What?!" Peter looked over at him again.

"Watch the road," said Louis. "You didn't know?"

"No."

Louis snorted. "I thought you had investigated me. I have cancer. Prostate. I have a treatment. I need a week. Then we'll start again. Afterward."

"Afterward?" said Peter.

"Afterward," said Louis.

Zaharia tapped on the wall. There was someone new in the adjoining cell. Zaharia tapped the alphabet three times before he got an answer. *Zaharia*, he tapped. *Here one week.* He thought he knew how long he had been there. You could tell by the meals. They came twice a day. And the guards. They changed shifts regularly, probably every two hours. Once every morning he was taken from the cell to empty his slop bucket. He had been taken once for a shower. It was almost as good as having a clock.

Mahmoud, came the reply. *From Pakistan. This better.*

How?

One man, one cell, tapped Mahmoud. *Pakistan ten men, one cell.*

Why prison?

Moslem, tapped Mahmoud. *Why you?*

Innocent, tapped Zaharia.

Ha ha, tapped Mahmoud. *Me too.*

Innocent, tapped Zaharia.

I was in Taliban school, tapped Mahmoud.

I was in school in USA. The sentence brought tears to Zaharia's eyes. Had he really been there? What had he done to end up here? Wherever here was. Why hadn't this terrible ordeal stopped? Where was Mr. Korngold? Where were Jennifer and Michael? Did they even know what had happened to him? And Granny Camille? And his mother? And Louis Morgon? Did anyone know or care?

Last guy here released, tapped Mahmoud.

Ahmed? tapped Zaharia.

Yes, tapped Mahmoud. *Sent home.*

Why? How?

Ahmed cooperated.

How?

Confessed.

Confessed what? tapped Zaharia.

Confessed crimes. Everything.

I am innocent, tapped Zaharia.

Then name somebody else, tapped Mahmoud.

Who?

Name somebody guilty.

Who?

Somebody not innocent.

Who? tapped Zaharia.

Somebody free while you here.

Who?

He is free because you are here.

Who?

Mahmoud did not answer.

Late that night Zaharia heard Mahmoud tapping. *Zaharia. I am so happy. I go home tomorrow. Free.*

Zaharia cried out. "No! No," he sobbed. "Please. How?! Why not me?!" When he had stopped sobbing, he tapped, *How you go home?*

I name friend, tapped Mahmoud. *Not real friend. He use me. I just boy.*

Zaharia stood facing the concrete wall. His eyes widened. Mahmoud was just like him. Then Zaharia recognized the deceit. He heard the tapping from next door, but he did not listen. He did not count the taps.

Be free, tapped Mahmoud. *Go home too.*

Zaharia did not answer.

VIII

Fareed Terzani sat on a stoop and watched some teenage boys burn cars. It was a chilly November night. There were maybe ten boys. They kicked the windows out of a car and splashed gasoline on the seats. When they threw a match, there was a loud whoosh, and the car was on fire. Flames leapt from the windows, and the windshield blew out. Flames exploded upward and met on the roof. They reached high into the air, giving off acrid, black smoke. One by one the tires melted. The car settled onto the asphalt, which melted into shiny, black pools.

In a few minutes six cars in a row were in various stages of burning. The night was lit up. The tall public housing buildings that lined the street glowed orange. This was the best they had ever looked. Sitting fifty meters away, Fareed could feel the heat from the fire on his face.

Sirens sounded in the distance. Fareed retreated inside. When the police arrived, the boys scattered. Some of the police gave chase on foot, but without success. The firemen sprayed the flames. A thousand empty windows looked out on the scene. No one was watching the spectacle. At least, no one the French police could see.

This was the third night of car burning. By now it was going on all over France. It had started right here in Clichy-sous-Bois, only twenty kilometers from downtown Paris. "Twenty kilometers and two centuries," Fareed liked to say. "Still," said Fareed, "burning cars is a waste of time. And a waste of cars."

Clichy had no Métro and no RER. There was only the 601AB bus, which made the long trip into the city carrying those lucky enough to work as hotel maids and dishwashers and gardeners. They dozed as they rode, or they stared at the black carcasses of cars from the night before.

Fareed Terzani was one of the fortunate among the fortunate. He had finished high school and then two years of technical school. He had been a good student and gotten good grades, especially in science, despite the roadblocks thrown up by bigoted teachers. By the time he was twenty, he had found an excellent job as a medical research technician at MicroBio Laboratories in Paris. His pay was good, and his boss, Alain Dupré, was a good boss.

Alain saw in Fareed a gifted researcher and a valuable collaborator. When Fareed needed to rearrange his work schedule in order to take more science courses, Alain gladly accommodated him. He helped Fareed decide which course of study would best advance his career.

When, after three years at MicroBio, Fareed decided to go to Tunisia, the country his parents had come from, and seek his fortune there, Alain Dupré was crestfallen. "I understand that you have to go," he said. "I would never try to hold you back. But I can't tell you how sorry I am to lose you. And, if you ever decide to come back, your old job will be waiting." A year later, when Fareed came back to Paris, Alain Dupré offered Fareed his old research job and raised his salary. Fareed had been at MicroBio ever since. It had been seven years.

Fareed had lived in Paris once, in the fourteenth arrondissement. He had a small, pleasant apartment off the boulevard Raspail not far from the MicroBio offices. But after a short time, he moved back to Clichy-sous-Bois, where he could go into shops without being treated rudely. He could walk the streets without being stared at or abused. And he could live near his parents, who were getting old.

Fareed's year away was not exactly as Monsieur Dupré believed, or as Fareed's parents believed, for that matter. "Maybe I can start my own research laboratory," he had said by way of explanation. But on landing in Tunis, Fareed bought a ticket to continue on to Karachi, Pakistan. From the Karachi airport, he took a taxicab to an address he had been given. Fareed spoke no Urdu, or any of the other languages of Pakistan, but he had learned the address phonetically, and the driver understood him.

The taxi stopped in front of a plain brick building with a thick paneled door and small, barred windows high up the front wall. When Fareed knocked and the door opened, he spoke a name he had also memorized. He was led through a courtyard where teenagers sat rocking in place and reciting the Koran. He was shown into a small room, which served as the school's office.

The drive from Karachi to Peshawar took three days, including stops to make repairs to the van and to visit the driver's family. There were six men in the van, plus the driver. Fareed was the only Frenchman. After two days in a hostel in Peshawar, the six were picked up and driven away in two cars. At the end of the road, they got out and walked. Horses carried their baggage and supplies. Fareed was astonished by the landscape. He imagined that the moon was something like this. After two days on foot, the jagged mountains opened into a small, deep valley with a river rushing through it.

By night, Fareed and the others slept in shallow caves that had been cut into the hillside above the river. By day, they learned to shoot weapons and handle explosives. They ran over obstacle courses and learned to communicate with one another without giving themselves away. They studied what their teachers referred to as the necessary arts and sciences of Holy War. They listened to lectures on the evils of the Saudi princes, on the American pursuit of world hegemony, on the Zionist domination of the Holy Lands, and other great wrongs that needed righting.

When his training was finished, Fareed was asked to stay on as a trainer. Osama bin Laden and his lieutenants had been watching him, and wanted to watch him a little longer. As Alain Dupré had before him, Osama now saw in Fareed Terzani an extraordinary young man. Fareed was intelligent, and he was an independent thinker. He had the perfect combination of talents to be a sleeper. He knew how to bide his time, make preparations for the task at hand, and ignore distractions.

Best of all, Fareed Terzani flew below the radar. A model citizen, educated, successful in a profession, he was unknown to police in France or anywhere else. He was not connected to any political organization. He was a perfectly blank slate.

After Fareed had been at the training camp for nearly a year, Osama sent him home to France. He was given a duplicate passport that showed he had never left France. "Do you have instructions for me?" said Fareed as he was about to leave.

"No," came the answer. "Except one."

"What is that?" said Fareed.

"Always fight the Holy War."

"The biopsies came back positive," said François. Louis's PSA had risen sufficiently in the latest test, so that even he had to admit that a biopsy was in order. "Eight of twelve cores are positive," said François. "That's a lot. It is well advanced. Cancer," he added, just in case Louis pretended not to understand.

Louis smiled.

"You're smiling," said François.

"I recently told someone I had cancer," said Louis. "I thought I was lying."

François shrugged. "Sometimes things we make up turn out to be true."

"I hope you're not going to start lecturing me about velocity," said Louis.

"What did Dr. Laférre-Benoit say?" said François.

"As if you didn't know," said Louis.

"So there's a consensus. The urologist, the surgeon, the oncologist. And me."

"A consensus."

"The surgery should be as soon as possible."

"How can I argue with a consensus?"

"You're smart to do it now. And Laférre-Benoit is one of the best. He's done it a thousand times."

"That kind of statistical reassurance always makes me nervous."

"Of course it does. You wouldn't be you if it didn't."

Louis took the train to Paris, where he checked into the Hôpital de Paris. He awoke after the surgery to find Pauline sitting at his bedside. Seeing that his eyes were open, she smiled and took his hand. "How are you feeling?" she said.

"All right," he said. He sounded surprised.

Dr. Laférre-Benoit came into the room. "It went perfectly. We'll see what the tests show."

"How old are you?" said Louis, frowning.

The doctor smiled, which made him look even younger. "Eleven," he said. "We'll keep you here a little while longer. We'll send you home once all the tests come back."

Two days later the doctor was back. "The cancer has not metastasized. There has been no invasion of your lymph nodes, bones, or any other part of your body. The bad news is that some cancer cells did escape the capsula of your prostate and were found in some of the surrounding tissue. Not a large area. But sufficient to warrant aggressive action.

"We're starting you on two drugs. They're designed to eliminate testosterone, which feeds cancer cells. These drugs will help suppress the cells. They may also slow you down."

"Slow me down?"

"Make you sick."

Louis frowned.

"It's good news," said Pauline.

"I still have cancer, and the treatment will make me sick," said Louis. "That's good news?"

"Stop feeling sorry for yourself," said Pauline. "You have some cancer cells. That's different from having cancer. It can be treated. He's doing it correctly."

"You sound like a doctor," said Louis.

"Old habits die hard. The chemo will be hard on you. It's hard on everyone."

"It comes at a bad moment," said Louis. "I have things I have to do."

Dr. Laférre-Benoit looked skeptical.

"He'll stay with me," said Pauline. "I'll watch him."

"Has anyone heard anything from Peter Sanchez?" said Louis. Before she could answer, he was asleep.

"He'll be like this for a while," said the doctor. Louis slept through most of the next two days. Eventually the grogginess left him. He started to eat. He got up and walked around Pauline's apartment with a stick, as he was supposed to. "What are the things you have to do?" said Pauline.

"I can't tell you," said Louis. "You shouldn't know."

"Is it always going to be like this, Louis?"

"I hope not," said Louis, and took her face between his hands.

Pauline frowned. When she went into her guest room the following morning, Louis was gone.

It had taken him a long time to make his way downstairs. The taxi he ordered was waiting. The driver stepped to the door and helped Louis into the cab. Louis gave the driver an address. The cab stopped in front of a bakery. "Wait here for five minutes, and then leave."

"*Oui, monsieur,*" said the driver.

The smell of fresh bread hung in the damp morning air. Louis went inside. "May I help you, monsieur?"

"May I have a *pain au chocolat*?" said Louis. He paid.

"May I use your back door to leave?" He held up the stick by way of explanation.

"Of course, monsieur," she said, and held the door for him. He walked down the alley and flagged down a taxi. He gave the driver an address in Clichy-sous-Bois.

Louis got out at Fareed Terzani's building. The street was empty except for a drunk passed out on a piece of cardboard beside the curb. His shoes were gone, and his pockets were inside out. The street was littered with trash, newspapers, plastic bags. A hungry dog rummaged through a pile of garbage, pulling out food wrappers. The building fronts, the fire doors, even the windows, the padlocked metal jalousie over the small grocery, the telephone boxes—which had no telephones—were covered with graffiti.

Louis went inside Fareed's building. He started up the stairs. *I'll be fine if I just take my time.* He braced himself on his stick and climbed to the first landing. He stopped to catch his breath.

Something was wrong. He felt his head go cold. Sweat was cascading down his face. His shirt was soaked. His pants too. He was dizzy and unable to stand. He sat down heavily on the metal stairs. He propped himself against the wall with his stick, so he wouldn't go tumbling down the stairs when he fainted.

"Monsieur, are you all right?"

"I just need a minute," said Louis, opening his eyes as wide as he could and trying to focus. "I'm all right." His head lolled back.

"You don't look so good." A young woman wearing a headscarf bent down and looked into his eyes.

"I'll be all right," said Louis.

"No, monsieur. Come with me. Stand up. That's it. Okay. Lean on my shoulder." In her apartment, Louis collapsed onto a sofa.

"Who's that?" said a man.

"He fell on the stairs."

"We better call someone," the man said. "An ambulance."

"Don't call anyone," said Louis.

"Drink this," said the man.

"What is it?"

"Orange juice."

Slowly Louis's head cleared. "Are you feeling better?" said the man.

"Yes," said Louis. "I just had an operation a few days ago. I think I overdid it."

He telephoned Pauline, and she arrived in a taxi. There was a man with her. He was tall with cropped white hair and black skin. "I'm Anwar," he said. "Pauline asked me to come along. Put your arm over my shoulder."

"Did you switch taxis, like I said?" said Louis.

"Don't you ever do that again," said Pauline. She stood on Louis's other side. Her chin was thrust out, and her green eyes flashed. "Ever!"

"Oh, yes," said Anwar with a laugh. "She gets mad. First time you've seen it?"

"Thank you for all your help," said Louis to the young couple.

Louis had to stay in bed. This time he did as he was told. When he was finally able, he returned to Clichy-sous-Bois. He knocked on the door of the woman's apartment. She peered out with the chain still hooked. Then she recognized Louis and smiled broadly. "Oh, how are you, monsieur? Come inside." She opened the door. "We've thought about you. We wondered how you were doing. Whether you were all right. I'm glad to see you looking so well."

"Thank you again for all your help," said Louis.

"Would you like a cup of tea?" she said. "I'm Natalie." She held out her hand.

"And I'm Louis." He took her small hand in his. "No tea, thank you."

"What brings you back here?" she said.

"I came to see one of your neighbors. That's all. That's why I was here in the first place."

"So early in the morning? Are you from the police?" she said. "That's what they do, you know. They come early in the morning. That way they catch people by surprise."

"The police? No, no. I'm just looking for someone, and I was hoping your neighbor could help me find him."

"Which neighbor?" said Natalie.

"I didn't see his name on the mailboxes. Some of the names are missing. Do you know all the neighbors?"

"Which neighbor?" said Natalie again.

"I'm sorry," said Louis. "His name is Fareed Terzani."

"Fareed? But . . . but you know him. You met him the other day. He gave you orange juice. Remember? He's my fiancé. We're engaged."

"Really?" said Louis, trying not to sound astonished. "Congratulations. That's wonderful."

"Well, who are you looking for? Maybe I know them."

"When do you expect Fareed back?" said Louis. "I'll just come back then."

"He'll be back this evening after work. He usually stops to see his parents on the way home. So make it after seven. Who is it, monsieur? Who is it you're looking for?"

"Zaharia Lefort."

Later Louis told Pauline about the encounter. "I couldn't very well say Osama bin Laden, could I?" he said. "I needed a name, so I gave Zaharia's. Of course the name meant nothing to Natalie, and I left. But, when I went back today, they were gone."

"So try again tomorrow," said Pauline.

"No," said Louis. "They're *gone*."

When Louis had gone back to Fareed's building, the stairway was filled with the sounds of televisions and babies and music. He smelled food cooking. Louis pressed his ear to Natalie's door. Then he knocked. There was no answer. He waited and knocked again.

The lock looked tampered with. But then, they all were in this building. He pressed down on the handle and felt the bolt moving, but not far enough to release the door. He pushed it back and forth. He studied the space between the jam and the door as he pressed the handle. He could see the bolt sliding and then catching.

Louis heard the sound of the television across the hall grow louder. The door across the hall had opened a crack, and an old woman was watching him.

"Have you seen . . . ?" he began.

"Gone," she said. "Gone. Gone!" She waved her arms.

"When?" he said. "When gone?"

Someone pulled her away from the door and closed it. He heard a bolt being slid shut and a chain being hooked. Louis knocked, but they did not answer. There were four other apartments on the landing. No one in any of them answered his knocks.

Louis went back to Natalie's door. He imagined eyes pressed against all the peepholes in the doors behind him. He moved the handle of Natalie's door a few times, then pressed it and pushed his shoulder hard against the door. The door popped open.

Louis studied the lock and the latch and saw that he was not the first person to get in without a key. The lock plate, which was supposed to catch the bolt, was broken. A narrow shard of metal had offered the only resistance to Louis's shoulder. He bent the shard back into place so it would hold the door closed.

The apartment had been ransacked. Drawers were pulled

out and overturned. Wastebaskets had been dumped out onto the floor. A computer monitor and keyboard were on the kitchen table, but the computer was missing. The clothes closets had been emptied onto the floor.

"I don't understand," said Pauline.

"I tipped my hand, and they ran," he said.

"Tipped your hand how?"

"I was too insistent about speaking just to Fareed."

"But where would they run?" said Pauline.

"That's the question," said Louis.

"And who came and ransacked the place?"

"Well, it could be thieves," said Louis. "That is the most likely scenario. Or it could be Peter Sanchez, although I doubt it. A mess like that doesn't sound like his style . . ." He paused suddenly.

"What is it?" said Pauline.

"Dimitrius," said Louis. "Phillip Dimitrius. The guy that was following me around Algiers."

"It's getting very complicated," said Pauline.

Louis smiled. "If you only knew. I need to find Fareed before Dimitrius does. Or Sanchez, for that matter."

"What about his parents?" said Pauline.

"His parents?"

"Remember? You said Natalie talked about Fareed visiting his parents on his way home. That means they are probably nearby."

Louis kissed her. "Thank you," he said.

"I'm still angry," she said.

The next morning, Louis was vomiting again. His face looked gray. He couldn't sit up without feeling dizzy.

"I'll go," said Pauline.

"No," said Louis. "Not to Clichy. Not alone."

"All right," said Pauline. "I won't go alone." She telephoned Anwar. She was waiting on the street when he drove up.

"So who is this guy, this Louis?" said Anwar as they drove across the boulevard de Port Royale. "He seems like an ordinary fellow."

"Yes, he does," said Pauline. "He's American, but he's lived in Saint Leon—not far from Marianne—for a long time. About forty years, in fact. He was a professor, then he was with the American government, the CIA. He retired. He moved to France. He gardens, he reads, he walks."

"Ah," said Anwar, "he walks."

"You're right. That was the first thing I liked about him. He also paints. And he's good at it. Landscapes, portraits, still lifes. All the outmoded, discredited forms. That's his style. He's contrary as hell.

"He's studied the masters, experimented with color, learned to draw. You can tell he's done the work. The paintings look ordinary at first, but they have an oddly surreal, almost haunted quality about them. A little like him."

"So, you're smitten," said Anwar.

"I don't know," said Pauline. "Are people our age smitten?"

"Apparently so," said Anwar. "I'm glad to see you happy. It's been too long coming."

"Thank you, Anwar."

"So what's this errand we're on? What's this all about?"

"It's a complicated story. I don't know much about it. Our part is simply to find a couple named Terzani, and to try to find out from them where their son has gone."

"And do you have an address?"

"No. That's what makes it tricky. No address. I have a street in Clichy-sous-Bois, where their son was living until recently. Louis thinks the parents live near the son, maybe on the same street. But it's a public housing neighborhood. There are probably a thousand apartments just on that one block."

Anwar glanced at his watch. "I've only got a couple of hours. I've got office hours starting at three."

"I think we'll either find them quickly," said Pauline, "or we won't find them at all."

"So what's the plan?" said Anwar.

"We start at a small grocery. It's the only grocery around. Everyone who lives nearby will have to come there eventually."

"You're good at this," said Anwar.

"It was Louis's suggestion."

There were people out and about. A few men, but mostly women carrying shopping bags. The grocery store was open, and crates of fruits and vegetables had been set up out front with prices written in chalk on slates. Arabic publications and strips of lottery tickets hung in racks in the windows.

"Wait here," said Anwar. "I have an idea." He got out of the car.

Pauline watched him stride across the street and disappear into the store. A minute or two later he emerged with the shopkeeper. The shopkeeper turned around, pointed up at his building, and then made a motion indicating the backside of the building. Anwar shook the man's hand. The man held on to Anwar's hand and used his other hand to point to his own elbow. Anwar spoke to him, and he released Anwar's hand. The two waved at each other, and Anwar came back across the street.

"What did you find out?" said Pauline.

"They live on the next street in a building exactly behind that one. The fourth floor."

"How . . . ?"

"I told him I was Dr. Anwar Mamdami—which I am. And I told him I had urgent business with the Terzanis, but that my knowledge of their address was incomplete. Which is also true."

"And all that business at the end?"

"He has a sore elbow. I suggested glucosamine."

IX

Abdul and Fatima Terzani opened their front door together. Abdul wore felt slippers and a dark gray wool suit over a light sweater. He had a small, neatly clipped mustache. Fatima wore a blue flowered dress that reached to the floor, and a dark blue headscarf. She had a round face. Her large, gray eyes all but disappeared behind her cheeks when she smiled.

Pauline and Anwar said they were medical doctors and were trying to find Fareed so they could speak to him. The Terzanis invited the doctors in. "Welcome to our home," said Abdul. "Please sit down."

The sofa and the chairs were all covered with protective sheets of plastic. The lampshades too. Fatima made tea while Abdul sat with the doctors. Every time anyone moved, the plastic rattled. Abdul looked at his hands, then smiled at the doctors, then looked back at his hands. They could hear the water running and the cups being set on the saucers. Finally, the teakettle was singing. Fatima brought the tea on a plastic tray. She poured it into the cups.

"Have you come to talk to Fareed about his work?" said Abdul.

"Yes," said Anwar. "About his work."

"He was called away," said Fatima. "It is something very important. A long trip." Her French had a heavy North African burr. Tears filled her eyes.

"She does not like it when he goes," said Abdul. He turned to Fatima. "You knew it would happen, that he would have to go again." He spoke harshly. She looked down and said nothing. He turned to face Pauline and Anwar. "When you do important research, you have to be ready to seize the moment." He made a seizing motion with both hands. They were certain it was a phrase he had learned from his son.

"A big opportunity. He is a medical researcher," said the mother proudly.

"They know that," said Abdul. "They are doctors."

Fatima wiped the tears from her eyes and smiled. She had gold teeth Fareed had paid for.

"Where has he gone?" said Anwar. "A famous laboratory?"

"Yes, a famous laboratory," said Fatima.

"He was not allowed to say," said Abdul. He smiled faintly. "Important research on . . . infectious diseases. . . .

He explained it to me once, but I could not understand everything. But they would know at his office."

"At his office," said Pauline.

"MicroBio," said Abdul.

"In Paris," said Fatima, and smiled proudly.

The MicroBio offices were all frosted glass and brushed alu-
minum. They were situated on the top floor of an office building on the rue Jeanne d'Arc in the thirteenth arrondissement.
Alain Dupré, the founder and owner, welcomed Louis into his
office. He was proud of the business he had built from nothing, and was happy to talk about it.

Alain had spent several years in the United States getting a
medical degree, as well as a Ph.D. in microbiology, after which
time he had come back to Paris to start his own research
laboratory. "I had good offers in the U.S.," he explained, "a
couple of New York hospitals and several large research laboratories. But I missed Paris. I wanted to start here.

"It was a one-person operation for a year or so. But grad-
ually, as I built up a reliable clientele, I was able to take on
other researchers. Over the years, we have assembled an out-
standing team, and together we have developed MicroBio into
a top-notch boutique lab. We have fifteen employees and do
very specific blood and serum tests for various Paris hospitals
and clinics."

"Like PSA tests?" said Louis.

"Yes," said Alain. "PSA and other routine tests, but also more complex and delicate tests, including a whole array of DNA panels. Doing these tests is MicroBio's bread and butter. But our—I should say my—real interest is infectious diseases. We have been isolating pathogens and trying to breed them . . . I don't know how much you know about microbiology."

"You've already exceeded my understanding," said Louis. "As I said, I am not a scientist. I am an investigator trying to locate Fareed Terzani."

"Fareed," said Alain. His face again took on a worried look. "He has not shown up for work for several days. I have called his number and gotten no answer. Not even his answering machine. Do you know where he is? I hope nothing has happened to him."

"I do not know where he is," said Louis. "I was hoping you could help me find him."

"Of course," said Alain. "I'll do anything I can to help. I want to make sure he is all right."

"Has he ever disappeared like this before?"

"Oh, no," said Alain. "It makes no sense. I can't understand it. It is simply not like Fareed. He's my most reliable employee. He would never leave without notifying me. Unless something has happened."

"What was he working on?"

"Mainly he has been working on infectious diseases. We all do."

"What does that mean? How does one 'work on' infectious diseases?"

"Well, we try to determine why they are infectious. How they are infectious. What their infectiousness consists of, so to say. How are they contracted, how are they passed on, and how can their infectiousness be interrupted?"

"And Fareed?"

"He was doing all of this on specific pathogens. This kind of research is quite common in microbiology labs. It is, after all, the prelude to every treatment for every infectious disease— every cure and every vaccine."

"And could this kind of work be the prelude to a *heightened* infectiousness, making something that is already infectious even more so?"

"Theoretically I suppose that is possible. But . . ."

"Was Fareed studying particular diseases?"

"He was interested in bacterial infections."

"Which ones?"

"Airborne infections. Wait a minute. Are you suggesting that Fareed . . . ? No, no. That is out of the question."

"Do you keep large stores of pathogens . . . here?" Louis looked around, as though a pathogen might be sneaking up behind him at that very moment.

Alain smiled. "No, we don't. In fact we have microscopic quantities which, for the most part, would not survive more than a few minutes out of their controlled environment. Most of our work is done using computer models."

"And none of your pathogens are missing?"

"They are checked each morning and each evening. No, none are missing."

"Where do you think he might have gone?" said Louis. "Had he talked about going anywhere to, say, do research? Conferences, other laboratories? That sort of thing?" Louis remembered something Abu Massad had said. "Did he ever talk about going to work in Berlin, say, or Copenhagen or Madrid or New York?"

"Well, he and I often talked of his going to New York. I wanted him to go there, to NYU, to finish school, get an advanced degree. He was interested. But he was also worried about his parents. 'Maybe someday,' he always said. 'Maybe someday.'" Alain shook his head.

"Did you or he ever have any contacts in or around New York in the course of your work?" said Louis.

"I did," said Alain. "All the time. I trade information with labs doing research similar to ours. But Fareed doesn't. That's not his responsibility. He is a researcher. That's not his job."

"But he could have," said Louis, "without your knowing it."

"I suppose so," said Alain. "But he wouldn't have."

"How many labs do you work with in the New York area?"

"There are four or five," said Alain.

"May I see Fareed's office?" said Louis.

"It's a lab really," said Alain.

The laboratory was small. A counter loaded with mysterious-looking instruments ran along two sides of the room. The only two things on the counter that Louis could identify were a pen and a pad of paper. He opened the drawers of the filing cabinets. The tab of each file was so meticulously labeled that Louis thought at first that the labels had been typed. He leafed through the files quickly but nothing caught his eye.

"That's Fareed," said Alain, admiring the lettered labels. "He is fastidious. He is neat."

Louis felt along under the counter. He felt under each drawer. He pushed the files to the front so he could look behind them and under them. He leafed through the files again.

"Could you turn on his computer, please?"

"Feel free," said Alain.

"I would if I knew how," said Louis. Alain stared at him incredulously. He turned on the computer. When Fareed's desktop came up, it gave nothing away.

"Would you like me to look something up?" said Alain.

"Does he have e-mail?" said Louis.

Alain gave him a look. Louis said, "If you show me how to search e-mail for particular words, then you can leave me for a while and get back to your work."

Alain leaned over the computer. "Type the words you're searching for here, click here, and you'll get a list of all the e-mails containing that word." Alain typed *New York,* and a long list of e-mails scrolled down the screen. "These are harmless," he said. "They're citations—footnotes, references. The computer finds every mention of New York, no matter how it was used."

"Thank you," said Louis. Louis searched for *labs, laboratories,* and *laboratory.* He looked for *pathogen* and *infectious* and *disease.* He looked for everything he could think of—even *al Qaeda* and *jihad.* Nothing came up.

"Newark," said Alain. He had stuck his head in the door. "I just remembered. Newark. He said he had a cousin in Newark who said he could stay with them if he ever went to New York." Louis typed in *Newark.* Nothing came up.

"You don't by chance know any names for the cousin," said Louis.

"No," said Alain. "Sorry. But I remember, Fareed liked the idea of staying in Newark. There's a good lab in Newark that is also working on airborne pathogens."

"What are these numbers?" said Louis, pointing to a vertical row of ten-digit numbers down the left side of the screen.

"Those are our case file numbers," said Alain.

"How do you arrive at your case file numbers?"

"The first two digits refer to a file drawer—an actual drawer—where paperwork from that file is stored. The next four digits are client numbers, and the last four digits are the actual file numbers. We just numbered the drawers sequentially. And filed things as the jobs came in."

"Why are the numbers out of sequence?"

"In the computer, the files are alphabetical by client."

"Is it possible to put them in numerical order?" said Louis.

"Of course," said Alain. He tapped a key and the files scrolled down the screen in numerical order.

"Astonishing," said Louis. He poked at the key he knew would scroll down the numbers. He stopped scrolling. "Do you notice anything about these numbers?" he said.

Alain wanted to find Fareed, but he was losing patience with this "investigator" who seemed to come from another planet.

"Ten digits," said Louis. "Like American telephone numbers. For instance, this number 21-2555-0498. Written differently—212-555-0498—this could be a telephone number in Manhattan."

"I see," said Alain. He sounded doubtful.

"There are ten 21-2 numbers," said Louis, "and eighteen 86-2—a Newark area code. Could we match them up with actual paper files?"

Alain sighed.

"I can do it if you need to get back to work," said Louis.

"No," said Alain, sighing again. "I'll do it." In a few minutes Louis had two stacks of files in front of him. He leafed through one after another.

Alain was gazing out the window. The day had turned cloudy. "What's this?" said Louis. He had a file folder labeled 86-2, but there were what appeared to be random sheets of paper in the file.

Alain scrolled down the computer list until he came to the number. "Intex Labs. That's the Newark laboratory I mentioned." He studied the computer file, then the paper file. "This makes no sense to me. There is nothing in this file that has anything to do with Intex."

"What is it?" said Louis.

"It looks like pages from a microbiology textbook. Fairly elementary stuff. Things Fareed knew. And some magazine pages. Why would he be keeping such stuff?"

"Maybe he just wanted to have something in the file." Louis wrote down the file number in his notebook. There was no way to break the news to Alain gently. "I'm sorry to tell you this, but Newark has two area codes. And New York City has five. I need to see quite a few more files." Louis handed Alain the list.

Louis got back to Pauline's apartment late that evening. Pauline wondered what he had found.

"Not much," said Louis.

"But something," said Pauline.

"Maybe," he said. "Five telephone numbers. Maybe. And some pages that may be significant. Only Fareed Terzani can say."

"Are you going to try the telephone numbers?"

"Maybe later. But not yet."

X

As a young man, Fareed Terzani had never known either doubt or desperation. Now he knew both. He had been living with doubt since September 11, 2001. The stunning assault on New York and Washington had come a year after his return from Pakistan, where he had learned how to plan and carry out exactly such operations.

Fareed's loathing for the Americans, the Saudis, the Zionists had been complete and unrelenting. But it was also entirely abstract. It was not linked to anyone or anything. It was a young man's rage, inchoate and unfocused. As was his conviction that only by destroying, from the ground up, the corruption those powers embodied—what Osama called Satanic powers—could the world be saved.

Fareed was not stupid. He recognized that Osama's language was symbolic. But he thought that he had lived through the truth behind the symbol. He had seen, growing up, how Abdul, his father, a well-read, educated man, could never find dignified work because his skin was dark and he was a Moslem. Abdul had ended up earning his modest wage wearing a bright green jacket and sweeping dog shit from the streets of Paris.

Fareed's mother, Fatima, went down to the grocery store, but not much farther. It had been years since she had been to Paris, although she had always loved to walk on the Champs-Élysée on a sunny Sunday afternoon. But the abuse and disrespect she had suffered—not always but often enough—since she and Abdul had arrived from Tunis now held her prisoner at home. She had been called names, laughed at, even spit on.

It is not difficult to understand how a young man like Fareed, who had witnessed the regular and unrelenting abuse and humiliation of his parents and others like them, might see in Osama bin Laden's violent uprising the only possible solution, the only way to banish such evil from the earth. Protect and uplift the downtrodden, feed and clothe the poor, heal the sick, and drive evil—Satan—from the earth. How could anyone argue with that?

Fareed was not a religious scholar. But he knew enough about the Holy Koran to understand that it was the will of God that the evildoers of the earth should be vanquished. And he was certain that all other religions had the same goal.

How could they not, and still call themselves religions? He had read about Jesus going into the Hebrew temples and driving out the moneychangers who were abusing God's house.

The trouble was that the twin monsters of money and power had infiltrated and ruined those religions. Now even Islam was in danger of being undermined by moral corruption and lassitude if something dramatic was not done. Striking the World Trade Center and the Pentagon seemed like the perfect act, striking as it did at the symbolic hearts of money and power.

That is where the doubt came in. Fareed turned on the television as soon as he heard that the attack was under way. The planes had already struck, but the towers were still standing. Fareed had had no part in this operation. Still, when he turned on the television he expected he would feel triumph and joy. Instead he felt horror and shame. He saw people leaping from the towers to their deaths in order to escape the terrible flames. Some of the people were on fire. He imagined his mother and father falling that way. People were running through the streets, burned people, people covered with ash, terrified people. People like him, like Abdul, like Fatima.

The people. He had forgotten that, whatever the World Trade Center and the Pentagon represented, they were filled with people. *How could I have forgotten that?* he wondered.

Alain Dupré was someone to be despised and destroyed according to the tenets of Osama bin Laden's Holy War. Alain was a Jew, which, in itself, was enough to place him beyond salvation. He owned a business and was, thus, just another greedy exploiter, a corrupt manipulator of bitter economic realities for his own selfish benefit. Except he wasn't. He wasn't any of that. He was a kind and generous man who had, for the last ten years, employed Fareed to do work that Fareed loved and found rewarding. It was purposeful, useful work, important work even, work that could eventually benefit all mankind.

Alain Dupré paid Fareed well for his work, and had done so from the start, so that Fareed now had a bank account with a substantial amount of money in it. Alain Dupré, a Jew, had treated Fareed Terzani, a Moslem, better than Fareed had ever seen any Moslem treat any Jew.

From September 11, 2001, onward, doubt was Fareed's constant companion. Fareed still had his assignment; that had not changed. The words *always fight the Holy War* rang in his ears. But he could not do it. He could not intentionally harm other people. He could not take research that could heal people and turn it around so that it would harm people. He could not. His doubt would not let him.

When he met Natalie, doubt became anchored permanently in his soul. He found that he could not admit the love he felt for her into his heart and, at the same time, admit the rage. They simply could not coexist. He felt tender toward Natalie. She was small and delicate and naïve. That was what astonished him most and what he loved best. She was naïve. She believed in the goodness of people. She believed in *his* goodness. Imagine that. *His* goodness.

Fareed had forgotten all about his own goodness. Natalie was so relentlessly kind to him, so patient with his dark moods and unexplained anguish, that she banished the rage and anchored the doubt forever. Louis Morgon would have said—maybe he *did* say it when he and Fareed finally met—doubt was salvation. Certainty was evil. Only doubt could save you.

The desperation arrived in Fareed's life the day Louis collapsed sick on his couch in Clichy-sous-Bois. It was not Louis per se. After all, Fareed had never laid eyes on him before. But there it was nevertheless. A dangerous stranger had found his way into Fareed's apartment by feigning illness. There could be no question about that. Louis was sent by Osama bin Laden to deal, once and for all, with Fareed Terzani, the reluctant, the doubting Holy Warrior, the traitor, the turncoat. The Holy War could not countenance doubt.

"I have to leave you," said Fareed. "I have to go away. He has come to kill me."

"What?!" said Natalie. "Why would he want to kill you?" She had never seen Fareed like this.

"You don't understand," said Fareed.

"No, I don't," said Natalie. "Why would he want to . . . ?" She tried to take Fareed's hand, but he pulled it away. "You're frightening me," she said. "Tell me what it is."

"The year I was in Tunis . . . ," he began.

"The year you were in Tunis?" Natalie tried to help him along.

"The year I was in Tunis," he tried again and stopped. "It made sense somehow," he said, "until I saw all those people on television." Natalie took his hand, and this time he let her. "The year I was in Tunis, I was not in Tunis," he said. Over the next hour, he told her the whole story. Natalie was astonished and appalled. But she was also relieved to discover the horrible truth behind Fareed's dark moods. And she loved him all the more, not because of his evil intentions, but because of the anguish those intentions had caused him.

"That is why I have to leave," he said.

"But how do you know who he is?" said Natalie.

"Who else could he be?" said Fareed. "Only jihadists know who I am, where I am. He must be one."

"Maybe he is just an old man who got sick on the stairs."

"He came back."

"Can't you just quit? Just give it all up? You just said it was up to you to organize your own action."

Fareed held his head between his hands. "Eventually an action must be organized. You can't just quit. It doesn't work that way." And Natalie and Fareed proceded to have more or less the same discussion Louis and Pauline had had after Peter Sanchez had showed up. "It doesn't work that way." "The world isn't as you wish it were." And so on.

"What about me?" said Natalie. "What about us?"

"This changes everything," said Fareed. "I can't ask you . . . I can't ask you to just . . ."

"You don't have to ask anything. This changes nothing," said Natalie. "At least nothing important. If you're going, I'm going with you."

"Your job . . ."

"I'm a waitress," said Natalie. "I'm going with you to . . . where?"

"Newark," said Fareed.

XI

When it came to concealment and subterfuge, Fareed was an innocent. Such things had never been part of his training in Afghanistan. He called his cousin in Newark to see whether he and Natalie could stay with them for a while. He called the Intex labs in Newark and arranged to come do research there. They knew of him from MicroBio and were happy to help expedite a visa for someone with his skills.

Fareed knew, of course, that the telephone calls, the expedited application, the record, including videotape, of him picking up the visa, all of it would be in the American computers. But, rightly or wrongly, he was not worried about the Americans, never having done anything to attract their attention. He was worried about the al Qaeda assassin, the old man with unruly white hair who called himself Louis Morgon and who was coming to kill him.

Fareed and Natalie waited in line in the customs building at John F. Kennedy International Airport. A customs official scanned his passport. It was the clean one that showed nothing of his having been in Tunisia or Pakistan. The official pointed to the camera and Fareed and then Natalie gazed up into it. Fareed's cousin, Lillian—actually she was his mother Fatima's cousin—was waiting in the crowded reception area. Fareed did not see her right away, but she saw him.

"Yoo-hoo!" Lillian was tall and wide. She had Fatima's gray eyes and round cheeks, and a voice like a full brass band. "Yoo-hoo! Fareed!" she hollered. Fareed looked around in consternation. His surreptitious departure from Paris had been compromised to begin with, and now it was on the verge of becoming a matter of public record. "Come here, you," said Lillian, and enveloped Fareed in a big, bosomy embrace. "Oh, I would have recognized you anywhere. And Natalie? Look at you, you sweet thing. Come here, sugar, and give Aunt Lillian a hug." All of this came out in a musical mixture of French, Arabic, and American.

"Say hello to Bobby," said Lillian, pushing Fareed and Bobby toward one another.

Bobby was dark brown and even larger than Lillian. His head was shaved. He wore sunglasses, a Fu Manchu mustache, and a gold stud in one ear. He looked ferocious, until he smiled. Then his face lit up like the sun. "Hey, Fareed, how are you doing?" He gave Fareed a complicated in and out, back and forth handshake that Fareed found difficult to follow. "Hey, Natalie." He pronounced it *Natly*. Her hand disappeared into his enormous paw. "Give me those suitcases," he said, "and let's go home."

"Let's go through the city, Bobby. Give them the fifty-cent tour," said Lillian.

"Through Flatbush, over the Brooklyn Bridge, the Holland Tunnel?" said Bobby.

"Perfect," said Lillian.

Fareed and Natalie rode in the enormous backseat of Bobby's ancient Cadillac, their heads swiveling this way and that, as they passed through the wonders that were New York.

"There's where the World Trade Center was," said Lillian.

Cars crowded from ten lanes into two and squeezed through the Holland Tunnel, fanning out in different directions on the other side.

"Statue of Liberty," said Bobby and pointed.

"Newark," he said as they left the New Jersey Turnpike.

Bobby and Lillian lived in half of a small duplex on Keyser Street in the city's First Ward. Keyser Street was two blocks long and tucked between the abandoned Bergen Industrial Canal and the Filipo Testaverde Public Housing project. It was a mix of single families and duplexes and assorted small businesses. There was a muffler shop next door, and farther down the street were a used furniture shop, Louie's Pizza, a video rental place, Mimi's Hair and Nails, and a liquor store.

Bobby parked by the fire hydrant in front of the house. "Go on in," said Lillian. She held open the gate of the cyclone fence. A large black and white dog came bounding around the side of the house. "That's Junior. He won't hurt you. Stay down, Junior!" Junior jumped up on Fareed. "Stay down, Junior," said Lillian.

"I'm gonna kick your ass, Junior," said Bobby. Junior jumped up on Bobby, and Bobby smiled his radiant smile.

"This was Felicia's room," said Lillian. "My youngest. She's up in Patterson. The bed's a little small. You stay as long as you want. Are you kids hungry?"

Lillian didn't wait for an answer. "Bobby!" she hollered. "Go down to Louie's and get a couple of pies."

Bobby hollered back, "What do you want on them, hon?"

"Double cheese. Bacon. The usual," said Lillian. "And get some Pepsi."

They sat at the kitchen table eating great slices of pizza and drinking Pepsi-Cola.

"It's good," said Fareed.

"It's good," said Natalie.

Lillian saw the exhaustion in their faces. "It's a long way from Tunis," she said in Arabic. "I've been here twenty-five years now. The first six months I hated it. Now I love it. It's not like Tunis. It's certainly not like Paris. But do you know what? Nobody cares what color you are, where you're from, what language you speak. Most people treat you decently." She switched to English. "Am I right, Bobby?"

"What's that, sugar?"

"Nobody cares what color you are."

"As long as your money's green," said Bobby, and grinned.

The Intex Laboratory was just off Orange Avenue and on the way to Newark airport's long-term parking, where Bobby worked. Bobby pulled into the Intex parking lot. "Here we are," he said. "That door sticks, Fareed. Just give it a kick."

Fareed watched the big Cadillac disappear down the street. Intex was in a windowless brick building. You pressed a buzzer to be admitted. Fareed buzzed and waited. The door buzzed, and the lock clicked open. He stepped inside.

"Yes?" said the receptionist.

"I am Fareed Terzani. I am a researcher. I called two days ago."

"Oh, yes," said the receptionist. She was chewing gum. "Have a seat. Mr. Blumenthal is on the phone. He'll be right with you." She stopped chewing long enough to take a sip from a soda can.

"Please come in," said Mr. Blumenthal.

Fareed sat down facing Mr. Blumenthal. "We're very pleased that you want to do research with us, Mr. Terzani. Mr. Dupré has spoken very highly—"

"You have spoken with Mr. Dupré?" said Fareed.

"Well, of course," said Mr. Blumenthal. "He has always

spoken very highly of you. And he seemed very glad—and relieved—to know that you were coming to work with us."

"But he cannot know I am here," said Fareed. "He must not . . ."

"I'm afraid it's too late for that," said Mr. Blumenthal. "When you called to say you were coming, I called him—"

"But I asked you not to call him . . ."

"I couldn't very well take you on, even temporarily, without knowing that you had left MicroBio on good terms."

"But I told you."

"I know, Fareed, but I had to check."

"I'm sorry, but I cannot work here. I cannot stay." Fareed jumped up and ran from the office. He ran across the parking lot and back up Orange Avenue in the direction of Keyser Street.

"He just bolted," said Arthur Blumenthal. He had telephoned Alain Dupré. "Is Fareed in some sort of trouble?"

"I think he must be," said Alain.

"What kind of trouble?" said Arthur Blumenthal. "When I said you knew he was here, he gave me a look like the devil was right behind him."

As far as Fareed was concerned, the devil *was* right behind him. "Are you in trouble, sweetie?" said Lillian after Fareed found his way back to Keyser Street.

Fareed did not answer but merely looked at the floor. "You have to tell them," said Natalie. "They will understand."

"They won't understand," said Fareed. "And even if they did, they could not help me. What could they do?"

"Talk to me, Fareed," said Lillian. Bobby was home from work. They were having supper. "If you're in trouble, boy, which you obviously are, then we've got to know."

"I can't tell you," said Fareed.

"Listen, Fareed," said Bobby. "You have to tell us. Or you have to move on."

"Bobby," said Lillian, but Bobby held up a huge hand. "No, sugar. We've got a right to know what we've gotten ourselves into. I haven't been mixed up in anything since I was a kid. I'm not going to get in trouble now, after all this time. So listen, Fareed. If you're in some kind of trouble, that's cool. We can live with that. We can understand. We can even help you work it out. But you have to level with us so we know what we're up against."

"Please, Fareed," said Natalie. "Tell them. They are good people."

Fareed looked at the three of them—Natalie, Lillian, Bobby. They waited. What choice did he have? He told them everything. He told them about training in Afghanistan with Osama bin Laden.

"Damn!" said Bobby. "Holy shit!" He and Lillian looked at each other.

Fareed told them about watching the towers burn and fall and how it changed everything for him.

"Uh-huh," said Lillian. "I know about that."

"But you can't quit al Qaeda, can you?" said Bobby. "It's like the Crips and Bloods. Once you're in, it isn't easy to quit."

"No, you can't quit," said Fareed. "And now they have sent somebody to kill me."

"And they know where you are?" said Lillian. "Oh, Lord have mercy."

"No, no," said Fareed. "They know I came to Newark, because Mr. Blumenthal talked to Mr. Dupré. But if I don't go near Intex, they don't know where to look. I told nobody I was coming to you."

"Nobody?"

"Nobody."

"Bobby?" Lillian looked at Bobby.

Bobby sat with a scowl on his face. He was chewing on his lower lip. His mustache twitched. His enormous arms were folded across his chest.

"Bobby?"

"I'm thinking, sugar."

The four sat in silence while Bobby thought. Their food sat half eaten and forgotten on the plates in front of them.

"You know anybody else here? In the U.S.?" said Bobby.

"No."

"You got any other contacts?"

Fareed looked at his hands. "I have some phone numbers. In New York City."

"Well, who is it, sweetie?" said Lillian.

"Al Qaeda."

"Lordy!" Lillian gasped and clasped her hands to her mouth. Bobby's eyes got wide. "Well, Jesus," he said. "We don't want to call them. Jee . . . sus! Stay away from New York, Fareed."

"Yes," said Fareed.

"You know what?" said Bobby. "I've got an idea."

"What's your idea?" said Lillian.

"Jamal," said Bobby.

"What about Jamal?" said Lillian. Jamal was Lillian's eldest.

"Fareed and Natalie can stay with Jamal," said Bobby.

"Bobby," said Lillian, "are you crazy? Jamal is a policeman."

"Exactly," said Bobby. "Who better than a policeman to protect somebody against al Qaeda?"

"He's been on the job less than a year," said Lillian.

"Jamal's got a legal gun, and he knows how to use it. And he's got the whole police force behind him. You think if al Qaeda comes looking, they'll want to fuck with the Newark police?"

"Sweetie . . . ," said Lillian.

"I'm telling you," said Bobby. "Listen, we get Fareed a job . . ."

"A *job?* A *JOB?!* Are you crazy?!"

"Now listen to me, honey. Listen to me." He laid his hand on her shoulder to calm her down. "There's an opening down at the long-term parking. Freddie's desperate to find somebody. It doesn't pay anything, but that doesn't matter. Money isn't the issue. I can work it out with Freddie. All Fareed's got to do is sit there and take people's money. It takes five minutes to learn. A smart guy like him, two minutes. I can get him hired. I'll be right nearby if he needs me. You find something for Natalie at Mimi's Hair and Nails. Then every night they go home to Jamal. And just like that, they're gone. Out of sight. And safe. Nobody will find them.

"Come on, you two, let's go see Jamal." Bobby was already on his feet. "Come on, Fareed. Come on, Natalie." He turned to Lillian. "You call that boy, sugar, and tell him we're on our way."

Jamal lived less than a mile away. He lived alone in a first-floor apartment. He shook hands with Fareed and Natalie. Bobby explained his plan and Jamal listened.

"Who's after them?" said Jamal.

Bobby explained. Jamal looked Fareed up and down. "Bobby, I've been on the force less than a year. This is a big thing, man. He should turn himself in. He'd be safer. They'd put him into protective custody."

"Jamal," said Bobby. "You know what kind of protective custody they put Arabs in? No offense, Fareed. You read the papers, Jamal. You watch the news. Guantánamo Bay, *that's* protective custody for a cat like Fareed. Anyway, I'm not asking you to do anything but let him and Natalie stay in your back room. It's not for long. Just until we figure something else out. Nothing's going to happen. Nobody's ever going to find them. You won't have to shoot anybody, Jamal. Relax."

XII

The Tigers had just beaten the Eagles. Joshua Sanchez had fumbled the ball, and that fumble had cost the Eagles the game. Peter walked with his arm over his son's shoulder. "It's a game, Josh," said Peter. "You did fine. It was a bad snap."

Josh tried to walk ahead. He wished his father weren't there. "You don't understand," he said.

Peter's phone rang. He took it from his shirt pocket and looked at the screen. "I've got to take this." Josh was happy he could walk on alone.

"Jesus, Louis, don't you ever sleep?"

"I need you in Cairo," said Louis. "I'm ready to start again."

"Really? How's your health?"

"Good. Good enough to go to Cairo."

"Cairo."

"Abu Massad was only the first name on your list. It led nowhere, so we move down to the next name."

"There's no need, Louis. It's over. We tried to get something going, and it didn't work. I know you're thinking you need to find something, to get some leverage to get Zaharia Lefort out. But it isn't like that. I'm working on it. It's not that far off."

"I need you in Cairo," said Louis. "Same place and time on the tenth."

"Louis," said Peter. "It's futile. It's ridiculous. It's not going anywhere. Stay home." But he was talking to a dial tone.

Anwar and Pauline drove Louis to Saint Leon. Anwar drove back to Paris, but Pauline stayed with Louis. The following morning, Renard rapped lightly on Louis's door. "Come in," said Louis. Renard opened the door and tiptoed into the room. He held a pot of violets in front of him like a religious offering.

Louis was sitting on the couch reading. He gave the policeman a puzzled look. "You're a little early for the wake."

"These are from Isabelle," said Renard.

Louis got up and carried the violets to the windowsill. He still leaned on his cane. He moved gingerly. "Should you be up and about?" said Renard.

"The surgery was almost two weeks ago. I *should* be playing tennis."

"Didn't they split you open stem to stern?"

"A couple of one-centimeter openings. They use scopes and robots these days. They hardly need doctors anymore."

"Let's have some coffee," said Renard.

"Tea," said Louis. He put water on the stove.

"What have you heard from Peter Sanchez?" said Renard.

"I'm sending him to Cairo," said Louis.

"*You're* sending *him*?"

"I have a peculiar hold on him." Louis smiled. It was a haggard smile. But it was a smile, and the policeman was glad to see it. "I told him to meet me there."

"You're going back to Cairo?"

"No, I'm going to Newark. That's why I want Sanchez in Cairo. I need to get him out of the way, to give myself elbow room. And then there's Dimitrius. I don't quite know what to do about him. Remember, I told you about him following me in Algiers? I think he's still snooping around and muddying the waters."

"I thought you liked for the waters to be muddied."

"I like to do it myself."

"Why don't you send *him* somewhere?"

"What an interesting idea," said Louis. He smiled again.

"And Newark?"

"Outside New York City, in the state of New Jersey."

"I know where it is," said Renard. "I just don't know what's there, why you're going."

"Neither do I exactly," said Louis. "I don't know much of

anything." He counted off the levels of his journey so far on his fingers. "First, Giorgio Smarth—whose connections are dubious at best—led me to Abu Massad. Then Abu Massad—who may or may not know anything—gave me the name of Fareed Terzani—who may or may not know something useful about al Qaeda. In any case, I scared Fareed Terzani, and he fled. To Newark."

"That's a lot of maybes."

Louis went into the bathroom and closed the door. Renard heard him vomiting.

Louis's recovery had not gone as the doctors would have liked. He was weak. The chemotherapy still caused him to be violently ill. His face had a wan and hollow look.

"You have an infection," said François. He took his stethoscope from his ears. He had come to Louis's house. "May I?" he said, and sat down on the chair beside Louis's bed.

"A pathogen?" said Louis.

François gave him a puzzled look.

"It's just a word I've come across," said Louis. "How did I get an infection?"

"Probably at the hospital."

"The hospital?"

"It's full of sick people," said François.

"You got me on the medical merry-go-round," said Louis. "Now get me off."

"I'm going to put you on a course of antibiotics. One every day, for three weeks." He reached into his black bag. "Here are a few to get you started."

"Can I travel?"

François gave Louis a withering look.

"I've got an important trip," said Louis.

"Where?"

"I can't tell you."

"So you're a spy again? Do you want to get off the medical merry-go-round, or not?"

"Yes."

"Then do as I say. Antibiotics for three weeks . . ."

"A course."

"And a course of acidophilus at the same time . . ."

Louis said nothing.

"What, no wisecracks?"

Louis said nothing.

"And rest. Stay home. Walk a little, but don't overdo it. Mainly rest."

Louis did as he was told. Pauline saw to that. He took the antibiotics and the acidophilus faithfully. He went to bed early. She often sat in the chair beside his bed until he fell asleep. She watched as he breathed deeply. The covers rose and fell across his chest. He slept deeply, and still his brow was furrowed. *He has led a life I can only imagine,* she thought. *Can I ever know him? What exactly is it that I love?*

A few days later, Peter Sanchez called.

Pauline brought the phone to Louis's bed. "Do you want to talk to him?" she said.

Louis took the phone. "What do you want?" he said.

"Zaharia is being released," said Peter. "I've found him. It will take a few days, but he'll be released soon."

Louis said nothing.

"He's fine," said Peter. "He hasn't been tortured."

"How do you know?" said Louis.

"He's fine," said Peter.

"What do you mean by 'a few days'?" said Louis.

"You know how these things work . . ."

"And what do you want from me?"

"Nothing," said Peter. "Your visit to Cairo is unnecessary. Our 'project' is done. How are you feeling? How did your surgery go?"

"You don't know?" said Louis. "You haven't studied the files?"

"I only know what you told me," said Peter.

"I'm still going to Cairo," said Louis.

Peter was silent for a long moment. "You know, Louis," he said, "it's good to be suspicious. Especially in our trade. But suspicion can also poison your mind. Some things you know, and other things you don't know. The trouble is, you can't always distinguish between what you know and what you don't know. So, if you want to doubt everything, fine. But if you doubt *every*thing, then you don't know *any*thing."

"I'm still going to Cairo," said Louis. "I'll see you on the tenth."

"I'll call you again when I know more about Zaharia's release," said Peter. He hung up the phone. He sat at his desk looking out at the bare, black trees. A few snowflakes were falling, the first of the winter. He went out to his assistant's office. "Book me a flight for Cairo on the eighth. Make the return open-ended. And get me a suite at the Ramses."

"What should I say if anyone asks?" said the assistant.

"Don't say anything to anyone," said Peter.

"Louis Morgon?" said the assistant.

"*Nothing to anyone*," said Peter. He went into his office and closed the door.

The day was sunny and cold. Louis took a walk. He left his stick at home. He walked between Pauline and Renard. Walking felt wonderful. He felt the urge to keep putting one foot in front of the other until the end of time. He linked his arms through Renard's and Pauline's. His cheeks got pink, and his skin tingled. Still, he got tired after a half hour. He took his breath in deep gulps. "Let's go back," he said.

"Do you believe Peter Sanchez?" said Renard.

"I don't know," said Louis.

"Why would he lie about Zaharia being released?" said Renard. "What does he possibly gain from that?"

Louis stopped walking. They were on a little bridge that crossed the Dême. He leaned on the iron railing and peered into the stream. Ice was forming along the bank. The water gurgled as it passed under the ice. It caused the daggerlike ice crystals to glisten and shimmer. Once in a while, a little silver dagger would break off and tumble downstream. "Sanchez gave me a little lecture about how suspicion can destroy me. He's right. It can. Maybe it already has. But I'm still suspicious." He smiled. "I have to ask myself, why that particular lecture at this particular moment?"

"Maybe he's concerned," said Renard.

"Maybe he *likes* you," said Pauline.

"I certainly hope I haven't given him any reason to like me." All three laughed.

"You know," said Louis, "I've never been an interrogator. But I've watched it being done. All the while Sanchez was talking, I kept thinking about how, when fear isn't working for an interrogator, they'll try hope. Something like, 'Good news, Renard, your release papers are in the works. Here they are. See? In just a few days, you'll be back home in Saint Leon with Isabelle.'" Louis pushed an imaginary paper across an imaginary table. Renard stared at the space between Louis's hands.

"'There's just one small bit of information we still need

from you, the smallest detail really . . .' That's what Sanchez's news felt like to me. It gave my heart a little flutter of hope. That sort of hope, expertly delivered, can break a prisoner better than almost anything. It reminds him of everything he is missing. How everything he once had is gone. How his life is essentially over. How he only has to do one little thing, and he can have it all back."

Imprisonment is a physical state and a state of mind. The physical part of prison is unambiguous and clear. It amounts to a concrete cubicle. The mental part is labyrinthine and deep, and has impenetrable layers. Every prisoner becomes a student of his own imprisonment. He cannot avoid it. His imprisonment is with him night and day. He observes his own spirit, his soul, his physical body as they are diminished by the experience.

Zaharia was no exception, although, being barely out of childhood, his study of his situation was entirely intuitive and scattered. Its truths came like a sudden revelation without context or meaning.

Disbelief is almost always the first stage of imprisonment. Zaharia overcame his disbelief quickly. It did not amount to much. Perhaps his difficult childhood had prepared him to accept sudden waking nightmares as part of the everyday.

His disbelief was soon replaced by the persistent and undeniable reality of his three-meter-by-three-meter cell, of bad and meager food, of discomfort, of isolation, of torture, of loneliness. This was his new life, and he took careful inventory of it. He could do this, in part, because he was so young.

Next, Zaharia entertained the hopeful thoughts that everyone wrongly imprisoned entertains. *It is all a mistake. Someone will come and release me. It can't last much longer.* This phase also passed quickly. Logically, from Zaharia's point of view, there was really no reason to believe that his lot would improve. He banished the idea from his thoughts. The here and now was sufficiently enormous to last forever. If you waited for things to get better, you were courting insanity.

The trick, Zaharia decided, was to empty his mind of all expectations. Forget the passage of time altogether. Obliterate time. Let the hours pass into days. Let the days pass into weeks. Let the weeks pass into months. Let the months pass into years, if it came to that.

Even in a place without clocks or windows, and where the light was always on, forgetting time was not an easy thing to do. He would sit on the hard edge of his bed with his eyes closed and try to shut out all sensation—the stench of the slop bucket, the rotten straw, the taste of his teeth and gums, the burning flea bites—everything.

The trouble was that just beyond hope lay despair. And despair was different from hope. Despair arrived of its own accord, like an independent being. How had it arrived? One day it was just there. It lived in him, around him, on him. It gnawed at his spirit like an animal. And only a razor-thin sliver of blessed emptiness lay, like a no-man's-land, just beyond hope and just this side of despair. Zaharia embarked on a search for that sliver of territory.

Sometimes when the guards peered into his cell, they saw him standing on one foot with his eyes closed. He stood that way as long as they watched. Back in the barracks the guards would try it, but they couldn't do it for more than a few seconds without losing their balance.

Other times they saw him having an animated conversation with imaginary characters. One character he gave a low, menacing voice, the other a high and innocent one. When they saw him like that, the guards thought of their own children making up stories and acting them out. In those moments, Zaharia seemed most like the boy he was. Zaharia spoke excitedly and even laughed. He gestured to the characters who were seated beside him. He asked them questions and answered for them.

"And if you get out?"

"Even if they throw the doors wide open, I'm not leaving," said the deep, menacing voice. "I will always live here. I *love* it here." He gave a villainous laugh. This was Zaharia's voice of despair.

"But think of all the good things you're missing," he said in a high, almost silly voice. This was his version of the voice of hope.

"He's going crazy," said the guard to his sergeant. But Zaharia wasn't exactly going crazy. He was trying to put hope and despair in their proper place by making them characters in a bedtime story and thus rendering them as harmless as he was able. He was determined to do the same thing with whatever demons entered his cell. And he almost succeeded.

Zaharia's interrogation had slowed down, so that sometimes three or four days passed without his being called. Then, when he was finally called, it almost made him glad. He was glad when the guards entered his cell, when he was taken to the showers once a week and hosed off. Just to be around other humans. The torture had also mostly stopped, and when it happened, it seemed halfhearted. Zaharia wished he had something to tell them.

After he had been imprisoned for nearly a month by his reckoning—six weeks in actual fact—a new interrogator was put in charge. The man from Texas was gone. The same two torturers stood behind the new interrogator. They were always there, whether there was torture or not. There was a lot of water on the floor around the toilet, which Zaharia took as a sign that the interrogation today would be forceful.

The interrogator started off by asking Zaharia the same questions the man from Texas had asked at every interrogation session. Why did Zaharia hate America? Did he know all the innocent people he was causing to suffer? When had he joined al Qaeda? Did he know this man? Did he know that man? Had he ever been in Pakistan? Did he know Louis Morgon?

Zaharia no longer protested his innocence. He no longer

sought or offered explanations for anything, since none of the questions they asked touched him, except the one about Louis Morgon. When he was asked whether he knew Louis Morgon, he always said yes. Except this time. This time he said, "no."

Zaharia did not know why he said no. It might have been the new interrogator; it might have been boredom. The interrogator gave him a puzzled look, and Zaharia repeated himself. "No."

He waited for the two torturers to step forward and put his head in the toilet. Maybe this time they wouldn't let him up. Except they did not move. They stayed where they were.

The interrogator smiled. "No," he repeated, and wrote something on the pages in front of him. He studied Zaharia. "Zaharia," he said, "how old are you?"

Zaharia actually had to think before he could answer. "Almost seventeen."

"Really," said the man. He shook his head sadly. "I have a son. He's fifteen, almost sixteen. He likes video games. Do you like video games? I hate to even think of him being in a situation like yours. I can't imagine how you got caught up in all this. It must be a terrible mistake."

Zaharia did not respond.

The man smiled. "I know you can't possibly be a participant in any of the things that are written here." He smacked the sheet of paper in front of him with the back of his hand.

The man's high voice sounded like the silly voice of hope.

Do not respond to the voice of hope, Zaharia told himself. *Do not listen to the voice of hope.*

"This information about you must be incorrect," said the man. "It can't be true. How can it be true? I don't believe it's true. Is it?"

Zaharia did not respond.

"I would like to send you home, Zaharia. We all would." Zaharia looked at the two torturers standing there. Did *they* really want to send him home?

Zaharia did not respond.

"I believe that you are innocent of any wrongdoing, Zaharia. I don't believe you did anything wrong."

"Then why don't you send me home?" said Zaharia. He was sorry he had spoken as soon as the words were out of his mouth. There had been a pleading note in his voice. He could feel the dam of his resolve giving way. And so, he was certain, could the interrogator.

"We're going to, Zaharia. We're going to send you home."

"When?" said Zaharia. Then, before the man could speak, Zaharia answered his own question. "I know," he said. "As soon as," he said. "As soon as. Am I right?"

Zaharia was taken back to his cell. The next morning he was taken from his cell back to the interrogation room. Only the two torturers were there. Zaharia's head was shoved into the toilet. That was the moment he resolved to die.

He did not struggle. Instead he breathed in. The water burned his nose and throat. His body convulsed from the pain of drowning. The two men pulled his head out of the toilet. Zaharia lay on the floor choking and gagging and vomiting. One of the men pushed hard on Zaharia's chest a few times and water ran from his nose and mouth. When his body stopped jerking about, the two men stuck his head in the toilet again. They had to make certain he was not pretending. Zaharia was carried back to his cell and laid on the bed.

Zaharia did not have a belt or shoestrings or anything else he could use to hang himself. Early in the morning, when he supposed the guards weren't looking, he lay with his back to the door and tore his pants into strips, which he quickly twisted into a rope. He stood on the edge of his bed and looped the short rope through the cage covering the light and then around his neck. He made sure it was tight. The door of the cell opened. The guards had been watching after all.

Still Zaharia hurled himself with force from the bed. The guards let him dance and choke for a while before they lifted him down and dropped him onto the bed.

When Zaharia woke up, he could not move his arms. They were in a heavy canvas harness that was strapped across his body and tied to the bed. His feet too were tied to the bed with canvas straps.

XIII

The sun was a silver disk low in the gray winter sky. It was cold in Saint Leon, but at least the wind was not blowing. Louis insisted on sitting outside. Pauline sat with him. They sat at the battered metal table with their backs to the house. Louis wore a heavy sweater and a shawl around his shoulders. They warmed their hands around cups of tea. Pauline was pleased to see that Louis's face had taken on more color. The infection had subsided, thanks to the antibiotics. "I feel better," said Louis.

"Good," said Pauline. "It shows."

"I feel stronger," said Louis.

"Good," said Pauline. "I can tell." She knew where this was leading. "You still need all your strength to deal with the effects of the chemotherapy."

"It's true, it knocks me out."

"It would knock anyone out."

"But I have to go . . ."

"I know you do," said Pauline.

"Soon," said Louis.

"When you're better," said Pauline.

"I'm well enough to travel," said Louis.

"I don't think you are."

"There's no other way," said Louis. "I'm better. I've waited too long already."

"Too long? A week?"

"A week in the life of a boy in prison," said Louis.

"I know," said Pauline. "But if you relapse in Newark you're no help to anyone, certainly not to Zaharia. Anyway, what do you expect to find in Newark?"

"I don't know. But something. I don't even know enough to know what to expect. Is Fareed Terzani an al Qaeda operative, as Abu Massad said, or is he the model citizen everyone else says he is?"

"Or is he both?"

"Or is he both? At least in Newark I'll find out. All I've found so far is a couple of peculiar file folders and a few possible phone numbers."

"And that's enough to take you there? If you go to Newark, how do you expect to find him?"

"Finding him will be easy. He went to the research laboratory there. I already know that. They called Alain Dupré and said he had been there. He's got a cousin in Newark. I've got names, addresses, and numbers. Fareed Terzani is not very good at hiding."

"If you go, then I will go with you."

Louis turned in his chair and looked at her. "Why?" he said.

"Maybe I can help," she said.

"You mean pick me up when I collapse? Hold my head when I vomit?"

"I may pick you up," she said. "But you'll have to vomit alone. And there will be other rules."

They took a hired car to the airport. They flew business class. Those were some of her rules. "It's a waste of money," said Louis.

"It is if you don't enjoy it," said Pauline. As if to demonstrate, she lowered her seatback and raised the footrest and took a nap.

Their passports were scrutinized and then scanned in the JFK customs hall.

A hired driver got their baggage from the carousel and drove them into Manhattan. Pauline had reserved a room at the Metropolitan Hotel on Fifth Avenue. They were on the eighteenth floor overlooking Central Park. "How much is this costing?" said Louis.

"Less than a hospital room," said Pauline.

Louis took off his clothes and went to bed. "Today is the fifth. Maybe we've got five days until Sanchez discovers I'm not in Cairo."

"And what if he finds out sooner?" said Pauline. She waited for his answer. But Louis was asleep. He slept deeply through the rest of the afternoon and through the night.

He woke up at seven thirty. The just-rising sun cast long shadows across the frosty park. The buildings on the west side of the park were orange and crimson in the early light. Puffs of magenta steam rose from their tops into the clear blue sky.

Pauline sat gazing into the park. The rising light shone through the cloud of her hair. It almost looked on fire. She turned when she heard Louis stirring. She smiled at him.

Pauline picked up the telephone and ordered breakfast. Louis could not recall that he had heard her speak English before. Breakfast arrived on a little cart a short while later. The plates were covered with gleaming silver domes. There was a shiny silver coffeepot, and a carafe of juice. Pauline lifted one of the domed covers to reveal eggs, bacon, potatoes. For the first time in a long time, Louis was ravenous. They sat at the small table by the window and ate.

Pauline looked up to see that Louis had stopped eating and was looking at her.

"What is it?" she said.

"It's you," he said. "Being here with me. I have been single-minded about Zaharia Lefort, about doing whatever I can to pursue his release."

"As I would expect you to be," she said.

"That's just it," he said. "That you would expect I would

be. I marvel that you would expect I would be, and that you would allow it without complaint."

Pauline laughed. "You know there are few Frenchmen who could come up with such a convoluted sentence as that. Your French is quite remarkable."

Now Louis laughed. "Well, appreciating the unexpected and the undeserved requires . . . convolutions. Is there such a word?"

"I don't know," said Pauline. She spoke in English. "But your single-mindedness in this matter is really something wonderful. I adore you for it."

Louis gave her a puzzled look. "Oddly enough, " Pauline said, "I find it easier to speak of matters of the heart in English. That is contrary to all the conventional wisdom, I know. But for me English is the language of love." Louis's eyebrows rose even higher. "Can you forgive me for that?"

They both rose laughing. They embraced each other. They lay down across the bed. Pauline's robe fell open. Louis kissed her up and down her body.

Later they dressed and went downstairs. As they walked across the lobby, Louis said, "I need to sit down. Over here."

They sat in side-by-side armchairs with their backs to the lobby. "Are you all right?" said Pauline.

"Perfectly," said Louis. "Look in the mirror." Pauline looked. "Do you see that man—keep facing me as though we're having a conversation—he's at about ten o'clock, reading a magazine."

"With the glasses? What about him?"

"He was on the plane with us."

"Are you sure? Who is he?"

"Phillip Dimitrius is my guess."

"Who?"

"He's the CIA agent who's been following me. According to Sanchez, he's the one who got Zaharia arrested. I do not know whether that is true or whether they are working in concert."

"Why don't you ask him?"

Louis smiled at her. "I may have to," he said. "Eventually. First, though, we've got to get rid of him."

Phillip Dimitrius watched over the top of his glasses while Pauline held Louis Morgon's arm and slowly walked him back to the elevator. A clerk came from behind the desk and took Louis's other arm. Louis had to stop more than once before they reached the elevator. Phillip watched while the elevator rose to the eighteenth floor.

After a reasonable length of time, Phillip Dimitrius rode the elevator to the eighteenth floor. A DO NOT DISTURB sign hung from Louis's door. Phillip pressed his ear to the door. The television was on. By the time Phillip returned to the lobby to resume his vigil, Louis and Pauline were in a cab bound for the Lincoln Tunnel.

As they neared the tunnel, the cab rolled to a stop, rolled forward, stopped and waited, then rolled forward again. Finally they were in the tunnel. Pauline leaned close to Louis. "Why is this Dimitrius following you?" she said. She spoke French.

Louis whispered in her ear. "He may believe I am a terrorist."

The French, thought the driver. *Even when they get old, they're still lovers.*

In Newark the driver found the Intex laboratory easily enough. Arthur Blumenthal told Louis everything he knew, but it wasn't very much. "Is it you Fareed is afraid of?" he asked.

"I don't know," said Louis. "Why? What did he tell you?"

"He didn't tell me anything. But he was terrified when he learned I had spoken with Alain Dupré."

"What exactly did he say?"

"Fareed said I shouldn't have told Alain that he was coming to Intex. He was terrified. He ran out of here like a shot."

"Has anyone been here looking for him?" said Louis. "Or asking questions?"

"No. Nobody."

Lillian looked through the curtains at the couple standing on the porch. They had already knocked twice. Junior had come running and barking. The man had immediately made friends with him. *Damn that dog.* Lillian decided to wait until they went away. Except they weren't going away.

The man sat down on the top step, and damned if Junior didn't lie down next to him and lay his big, stupid head right on the man's lap. The woman sat down next to the man on the other side. She put her hand on his back and asked him something. It sounded like French. The man was pretty old and didn't look in the best of health.

Lillian opened the door. "May I ask what you folks are doing on my porch?" The man got to his feet as best he could. The lady helped him up. They were neither one of them spring chickens. "Can I help you with something?"

"I apologize if we startled you," said the man. "I knocked, but you must not have heard it."

I heard it, thought Lillian. *And you know I heard it.* "No, I guess I didn't," she said.

"My name is Louis and this is Pauline. It is very urgent that we speak with Fareed Terzani."

Oh my God, thought Lillian. *It's them. It's al Qaeda. Except, look at them. They don't look like they could harm a soul.* "Who?" she said.

"Fareed Terzani," said Louis.

"Fareed?" said Lillian. "I don't know any Fareed."

"Well," said Louis, and he shrugged. "Where else would he go? You're his cousin, after all. Isn't Fatima Terzani your cousin? And Fareed is her son."

"There's no one named Fareed here," said Lillian. "Now you folks are going to have to get off my porch."

"It is very important that I speak with Fareed," said Louis. "His life may be in danger."

"Uh-huh," said Lillian. "*Your* life may be in danger if you don't get off my porch." She reached for the baseball bat she kept by the door. She made certain that Louis saw it.

"Madame," said Pauline, "do you speak French?"

"Yeah," said Lillian. "A little. Why?"

"Because," said Pauline in French, "my English is not very good. Please, madame, Monsieur Morgon and I—I am Pauline Vasiltschenko—we understand you are protecting your cousin. But if we know he is here, then others do too."

"He isn't here," said Lillian.

"We are leaving, madame," said Pauline. "But please tell Fareed it is important to him that we meet. We will meet with him anywhere and under any circumstances he prefers. We will return tomorrow morning at the same time." She took Louis's arm. Junior trotted with them to the gate. Lillian watched them walk up Keyser Street.

The following morning, Louis and Pauline parked their rental car in front of Mimi's Hair and Nails and walked to Bobby and Lillian's house. Bobby was waiting on the porch. He stood with his arms crossed on his chest and watched them approach. Junior was nowhere in sight.

"May we come in?" said Louis, his hand on the gate. "We're not armed."

"It doesn't matter if you are," said Bobby. "There's a Newark policeman inside that window with his shotgun aimed right at your head."

Louis opened the gate, and he and Pauline walked through.

"That's far enough," said Bobby. "Now, who are you and what do you want?"

Louis told him, as briefly as he could. He explained that he, Louis, had a bad history with the CIA. He explained how Zaharia had been kidnapped, and how he was looking for something to trade for Zaharia's release.

"You're looking to trade Fareed for your boy?" said Bobby.

"Is Fareed with al Qaeda?" said Louis.

Bobby considered how he wanted to answer that. "No," he said finally. "But he knows something about them."

Now it was Louis's turn to consider. "What I need is what he knows," he said.

"And what are you offering?" said Bobby.

"The CIA is right behind me—a man named Phillip Dimitrius and another one named Peter Sanchez. It's only a matter of time—a day or two, at most—until they find him. I don't know whether they're working together or not. But what I'm offering Fareed—and Natalie—is the chance to be safe."

"We can keep Fareed safe all right," said Bobby. "So, the way I see it, you're offering nothing."

Louis narrowed his eyes and took a step toward Bobby. Bobby took a deep breath. He seemed to get even bigger. "I can see you're a smart man," said Louis. "And I don't doubt your seriousness of purpose. Or your strength. But I can find Fareed in a few hours by myself.

"I know you work at the airport—the sticker on your bumper tells me that. I know you've got a friend, or relative, on the police force." Louis nodded his head toward the house. "You told me that yourself. So, if I follow you, or him"—Louis nodded toward the house again—"I'm guessing I'll find Fareed. Don't take this the wrong way, but this is my line of work. And it's not yours. If you hide Fareed really well, it will still only take me a day or two to find him. The same goes for the CIA guys.

"Now, think about this," Louis continued. "You have to know by now that I mean Fareed no harm. I gave you a full day's notice I was coming back. If I was going to harm Fareed, would I have done that? I want to meet him on terms of mutual trust and understanding. If it's not done that way, it just won't work. However you want to arrange and organize the meeting is fine with me. All I would suggest is that you make it happen sooner rather than later. For Fareed's sake."

Bobby chewed vigorously on his lip. His mustache twitched from side to side. "Wait here," he said. He went inside.

"Did you hear all that?" he said.

"Most of it," said Lillian.

"Yeah," said Jamal. He lowered the shotgun, but he continued to watch through the window.

"What do you all think?" said Bobby.

"I don't know," said Lillian. "It all sounds too crazy to be made up."

"He's a cool number," said Jamal. "Damn. The way he came through that gate. And what about the lady?"

"She doesn't say anything," said Bobby.

"She's French," said Lillian. "The man's not in good shape. She may be along just to help him out. They sure don't seem like al Qaeda to me."

"What he said about coming back and not hurting Fareed and all," said Bobby, "that makes sense."

"To me too," said Jamal. "And the way he found Fareed. He'd find him easily, wherever he is. The best thing you can do, Bobby, is have them meet where we can protect Fareed."

"So how do you do that?" said Lillian.

"It's got to be a place where we're all alone," said Bobby, "where we can organize things, and where we're protected, Fareed is protected, and he's not."

"I've got just the place," said Jamal. "And just the protection. I need two, maybe three hours."

Bobby went back outside. "Okay," he said. "Here's what we'll do. We'll take you to a meeting with Fareed three hours from now. But you can't go anywhere between now and then. You stay right here where we can see you the whole time."

"Fine," said Louis.

"Could you bring him a chair?" said Pauline.

Bobby brought out two chairs. "You need some water or something?" he asked.

"Could you let your dog out while we wait?" said Louis.

"Junior?" said Bobby. "What for?"

"I like him," said Louis.

XIV

Jamal sat in the backseat of the Cadillac, and Louis sat beside him. Pauline sat in front, next to Bobby. Bobby headed down Keyser Street. After a few blocks, they crossed the Bergen canal on a black, iron bridge. The bridge rattled and groaned as they drove across. On the other side of the bridge, the landscape changed. Streets were crumbling, the sidewalks had mostly disintegrated. Junk sumac and locust trees grew up through cracks in the pavement. Trash was everywhere—tires, cardboard, cans, bottles. The plywood across the windows and doors of most of the houses was covered with grafitti. Abandoned cars with bashed-out windshields and missing wheels sat collapsed by the curb. In the distance, behind the houses, were rusting storage tanks and, farther back, a tall, black stack with a staircase spiraling up around the outside. A jet of yellow flame erupted from the top.

They passed the remains of a warehouse or factory. Every one of its hundreds of windowpanes had been broken out. Shards covered the sidewalk below. There were no people on the streets. It was as though the purpose of this place had been to be destroyed. That work was done and everyone had moved on to the next job.

Bobby stopped the car behind the remains of a small factory building made of yellow bricks. Its windows were gone.

A young black man leaned against the building beside its steel entry door. Jamal walked up to the man. They bumped fists and spoke briefly. Jamal signaled with his head.

"Let's go," said Bobby. "That door sticks," he said to Pauline. "You have to kick it."

The young man by the building wore low-riding, baggy jeans, blue sneakers, a black T-shirt, a Yankees hat cocked on his head, and a thick gold chain around his neck with gold letters that spelled EEK. He had prison tattoos on both arms. He did not indicate in any way that Louis or Pauline were even visible to him.

Jamal led the way inside and down a long corridor. They came to a large windowless room. There was a broad round concrete pit in the center of the room with a series of wide drains in its floor. Five more young black men sat on the edge of the pit with their legs dangling. Like the man at the door, they watched without watching. Jamal went from one to the next and bumped fists. No one spoke.

Jamal came back around the pit to Louis. "Sit here," he said. Louis and Pauline sat down on the edge of the pit. Bobby sat down beside Louis.

"I'll be right back," said Jamal.

When he came back, Fareed was with him. "Sit here," said Jamal. Fareed sat down on the edge of the pit so that Bobby and Jamal were between him and Louis in one direction, and the five young men were between him and Louis in the other.

"Who are you?" said Fareed. "And why are you following me?"

"My name is Louis Morgon. I am following you because I need your help."

"I do not believe you."

"I don't blame you," said Louis. "Let me explain." Louis told the story he had already told Bobby, about his CIA experience, about Zaharia. The five young men sat impassively as though he were talking in a language they did not understand.

Fareed listened intently. He leaned forward and kept his eyes on Louis. "How did you find me?" he said.

Louis explained that he had gotten Fareed's name from Abu Massad in Cairo. He explained that he had not been looking for Fareed particularly. He was looking for anyone he could use to effect Zaharia's release from prison. It just happened that

Fareed was the name Abu Massad gave him. "I don't know how or where he got your name, or why he gave it to me. I didn't ask."

"Why was the boy arrested?" said Fareed.

"They think he is a terrorist," said Louis.

"Why does the American government arrest innocent people?"

"They also arrest guilty people. In times like these, they are not very good at telling the innocent from the guilty. Nobody is. Everybody is too fearful to see things clearly."

"And so you are not from al Qaeda?"

"No," said Louis.

"You have not come to assassinate me?"

"Is that what you thought? Is that why you ran?"

"Of course," said Fareed. "Who else but al Qaeda could know about me? And now you want to trade me for this boy?"

"Tell me why I should not," said Louis. "Abu Massad, the man who gave me your name, said you are al Qaeda. And you have just said so yourself. Tell me why I should not trade your life for that of an innocent boy."

Fareed jumped to his feet. "But you are no different than they are," he shouted.

"I am completely different," said Louis. "I am talking with you. I am asking you questions."

Fareed's body slumped. He saw now that it did not matter

who this Louis Morgon character was, if that was even his real name. Whether he was an al Qaeda assassin or a CIA agent, it made no difference. Fareed's life as a free man was over. Maybe his life was over, period. He had trained with al Qaeda and had, in that long-ago act, condemned himself to prison or death by one hand or the other. CIA or Qaeda. It did not matter. Joining al Qaeda had been an irreversible and unforgivable act that had sealed his fate. Perhaps that was as it should be. Fareed dropped his face into his hands. Jamal stood up, and so did the five young men. "Say the word, Fareed, and this meeting is over," said Jamal.

Pauline was the last person anyone expected to hear from. And what she said was probably the last thing anyone expected to hear. In fact, her words did not even register at first. They fell into the center of the circle and reverberated in everyone's ears without making sense, as though someone had dropped a handful of ball bearings on the concrete floor and they were rolling around.

"Does al Qaeda believe in forgiveness?" she said. Everyone looked at the floor of the pit, where the ball bearings would have been.

Pauline had understood Fareed's panic. "Fareed," she said, speaking more slowly now. "Answer this one question. It is important. Does al Qaeda believe in forgiveness?"

"What?" said Fareed. He still did not understand what she was asking.

Pauline posed the question yet again. This time she said it in French. *Does al Qaeda believe in forgiveness?*

Was it that she was a woman? Perhaps she made Fareed think of Natalie, who was hidden somewhere, waiting anxiously with Lillian, wondering, not about her own fate, but about Fareed's. Natalie certainly knew about forgiveness. She had forgiven Fareed. Or maybe it was simply the sound of the French words, the sound of the language in which he had renounced violence and found happiness, Natalie's language. Whatever the reason, Fareed crossed his hands in front of him, and answered in a barely audible whisper, as though he were speaking some odd, new vow of renunciation. *"Non,"* he said, first in French, then in English. "No."

"And what about *you*, Fareed?" said Pauline. "Do *you* believe in forgiveness?"

"Yes," said Fareed.

"And you?" said Pauline. Louis looked at her in astonishment. She was talking to *him*. "Louis, do you believe in forgiveness?"

Louis had definitely not meant for things to go this way. The first rule for transactions like this was to shut out everything else. All feelings, all private agendas and business, preferences, likes and dislikes, everything had to be put aside. Certainly questions of forgiveness. The negotiation at hand was paramount. And yet, despite his best efforts, prompted by the completely unexpected turn of events, Louis felt his mind racing backward over his life, beyond Pauline, to Zaharia, to Solesme, to Jennifer and Michael, the children he had more or less abandoned, to Sarah, the wife he had left, to all those he had offended and harmed. They all rose in his mind's eye, like an army of the wronged.

He looked up at Pauline. "Forgiveness?"

"Yes," she said.

"Forgiveness is something I hope for every day," said Louis. "Without forgiveness . . ." He could not finish the thought.

The young men on the other side of the concrete basin sat back down and dangled their legs again. They watched without watching. Later Louis remarked to Pauline that these young men were like a Greek chorus in an ancient play, watching pitilessly while the pathetic and foolish mortals concocted yet another complicated ceremony to sort out what should have been a simple situation.

Jamal sat back down. So did Fareed. "Fareed," said Louis. "Can we talk?"

"Yes," said Fareed.

Louis withdrew some papers from his pocket and passed them to Bobby who handed them to Fareed. Fareed looked at the papers.

"These are from my lab at MicroBio," he said. He looked astonished. "They were hidden."

"Yes," said Louis. "And pretty well hidden too. What are they?"

"They are telephone numbers and encrypted computer codes," said Fareed.

"Telephone numbers?" said Louis.

"For Qaeda in New York, in New Jersey." The Greek chorus moved uneasily where they sat.

"And the computer codes?"

"Codes to gain access to the Qaeda communications net on the Internet."

"How does the encryption work?" said Louis.

"It uses the pages of a magazine," said Fareed. "You buy the current issue of a specified magazine, turn to a specified page. I can show you."

"What is encoded?"

"Internet addresses and then passwords that allow you to access Qaeda sites."

"In order to do what?"

"In my case, just get the updated codes. To stay current."

"In other cases?"

"To report actions, to make liaisons, to get instructions."

"You didn't report actions or make liaisons or get instructions?"

"I was a sleeper," said Fareed. "I was planted as an agent for some future action. It's different. I had no assignment. I was just waiting. I would have reported actions. But I had none to report."

"Why not?"

"Because I didn't do any actions."

"Why not?"

Fareed paused and looked at his hands. "Because I watched

the towers fall on September 11. I couldn't do that. It turned out I didn't hate anyone."

Louis gave Fareed a long, hard look. "Why were you afraid of al Qaeda? You were a sleeper. You could have lived out your life without ever doing anything."

"I panicked," said Fareed. "I don't know why. Are you going to turn me in to the CIA?"

Louis thought for a long moment. "I need you to verify the information you're giving me."

"I can do that," said Fareed.

"Then," said Louis, "I'm going to need you to meet with a man from the CIA."

"Why should I trust you?" said Fareed.

"You don't have to trust me. You only have to trust them." Louis made a gesture that took in everyone else in the room.

"I don't understand," said Fareed.

"Trust *them*," said Louis. "Because it's all going to happen right here. Or somewhere like this. We'll work that out to your satisfaction. And all your friends"—Louis indicated Bobby, Jamal, and the Greek chorus—"and anyone else you'd like to have present will be there to protect you."

The Greek chorus shifted once again. They glanced at one another and murmured softly.

In order to be as certain as he could be that Peter Sanchez would go to Cairo, Louis had bought himself an airline ticket for Cairo and reserved a rental car there. He had even booked a room at the Toledo. He could have saved himself the trouble, and the money. Peter Sanchez did not even check; he could not afford to stay home. There were still the who-the-hell-is-Peter-Sanchez stories that could end his career. And if Louis did turn up something in Cairo, which was by no means out of the question, given his resourcefulness, Peter had to be there.

Peter Sanchez departed Washington the afternoon of the eighth and arrived in Cairo the afternoon of the ninth. He went to the Ramses breakfast room the following morning. Louis did not appear. Peter did some checking. He was on his way to the Toledo when his telephone rang.

"I have something for you," said Louis.

"Where are you?" said Peter.

"I have something for you."

"It better be good," said Peter.

"If you are the first to get it, it will make you a hero. If you aren't, it will ruin your life."

"What are you talking about?" said Peter.

"Zaharia Lefort," said Louis.

"I told you, he's on his way out of prison. It's days away."

"Well then, that should make it easy for you," said Louis. "Bring Zaharia to New York. Restore his passport. Hand him to me. In return, I'll give you at least three al Qaeda cells in and around New York City. Cells that you know nothing about. I'll give you access codes for monitoring Qaeda communications. And subverting them if you're clever enough. And I'll give you an al Qaeda operative."

There was silence from Peter. Louis waited. "It doesn't work like that," said Peter finally. "I can't produce the boy just like that."

"Really?" said Louis. "Then you better find someone who can. If I don't get the boy, then the information and the informant, everything, goes away."

"You would do that?" said Peter Sanchez. "You would jeopardize the security of your country like that? You would risk the lives of thousands of innocent American citizens, just because you can't have your way?"

"Sanctimony doesn't suit you, Peter." It was the first time Louis had ever called him by name. "And sanctimony doesn't work on me. New York on the fifteenth. That's a gift. It gives you four more days. I'll call you that morning to set up the meeting that afternoon." Louis hung up the phone.

"Son of a bitch!" said Peter. "Stop the cab," he said to the driver. When the driver didn't stop immediately, Peter shouted at him. "*Stop the goddamn cab.*" Peter instructed the driver to return to the Ramses immediately.

The square ahead was jammed with buses, cars, and trucks. The air was filled with blue fumes. Horns honked. People shouted. Teenage boys jumped from the back of the buses where they had been hitching a ride. "Go that way," said Peter, pointing to an open side street. But, in fact, there was no way the driver could maneuver his cab in that direction. He shrugged and smiled helplessly into the rearview mirror. "Accident," he said.

It took an hour for Peter to get back to the Ramses. He could have walked it faster. His shirt was soaked in sweat. He had a headache. As he walked into the lobby, his telephone rang. He did not recognize the number on the screen.

"Hello," he said.

"Peter Sanchez?" said the voice. "This is Phillip Dimitrius."

"You're kidding," said Peter.

"No, sir," said Phillip Dimitrius.

"Why are you calling me?"

"I was told to call you when I got close," said Phillip.

"Close?"

"Yes, sir," said Phillip. "And I think I am. Finally."

"Where are you?"

"New York. The Metropolitan Hotel."

"And where is he?" Finally something was going right.

"He's staying here at the hotel. He's been spending time in Newark."

"You know where?"

"Yes, sir," said Phillip.

"Can you stay with him?" said Peter.

"Yes, sir."

"Have you seen him with anybody?"

"Besides the Frenchwoman?"

"Yes. Besides the Frenchwoman."

"There's a couple in Newark. A black dude and his Arab girlfriend."

"Who are they?"

"A black dude and his Arab . . ."

"Yes, I understood that. What's the connection?"

"She's an Arab . . ."

"All right. Here's what you do. Keep Morgon in sight. Don't lose him. Find out what you can about what he's up to. Don't let him know you're there."

"It's too late for that, sir. I don't know how he did it . . ."

"Jesus," said Peter.

"Sir?" said Dimitrius.

"Just stay with him," said Peter. "I'll be there as soon as I can."

XV

After a particularly unpleasant interrogation, Zaharia was taken to an office where he had never been before. He was allowed to sit on a chair. An American army officer stood in front of him. He stood with his arms crossed and studied Zaharia. Zaharia met his gaze without actually seeing him. The officer pulled a tissue from a box. He withdrew several more and handed them to Zaharia. He touched his upper lip, to signal where Zaharia should use the tissue. Zaharia dabbed at his lip, which was swollen and oozing blood.

"You're being transferred," the man said. "All you have to do is sign these papers." Zaharia tried to read the paper, but he could not focus on the words. "It's not a confession or anything," said the officer. "It just says that you were appropriately treated and that you waive all . . ." Zaharia stopped listening. The man pressed a pen into his hand and Zaharia signed. Zaharia's arms and legs were shackled. This had become routine. When they were not, he tried to harm himself.

A hood was placed over his head. Zaharia was escorted from the prison. He walked between two guards. Because of the shackles, he could only walk with a slow shuffle. But the guards were patient. Zaharia could see the ground from the bottom of the hood. He could smell the winter air and feel the cold on his skin. He was outside. The last time he had been outside it had been warm.

The guards walked him up three stairs onto a bus. One sat beside him; the other sat behind him. The bus drove for a long time. Zaharia fell asleep. He woke up when the bus stopped. His lip was throbbing. The two guards walked him down the stairs of the bus. They walked him up a long ramp. He could tell he was getting on an airplane. He was placed on a seat. Someone was sitting next to him but he did not think it was a guard. When he had to go to the bathroom a guard took him. After they had been flying for many hours he was given a cheese sandwich and a box of fruit juice. He sucked on the straw until the box collapsed. He kept sucking on the straw long after there was no more fruit juice, and they took the box away from him. Someone gave him another box of fruit juice. He drank it all. He slept.

He woke up as the hood was being removed from his head. He could see that he was one of only a few men riding as passengers in the large airplane. At least half of them were in uniform. He fell asleep again and slept until they landed.

Zaharia was put in a van. He saw an American flag waving as they left the airport. They drove on a highway beside a large body of water. The highway signs were in English. 55 MPH. NEW JERSEY TURNPIKE. In the distance across the water he glimpsed tall buildings. It was New York. They left New York behind and drove south. More signs. Zaharia read them aloud without knowing he was doing so. "IKEA. Elizabeth. Port facilities next exit." They drove past shipping docks with enormous stacks of shipping containers. They left the turnpike and drove on a series of side roads.

They drove past a guard house. A guard in civilian clothes and wearing dark glasses stepped out of a second small guard house and checked the papers the driver handed him. He waved them onto the base. The van stopped. A guard took Zaharia into a concrete building. He was put in a room. Zaharia knew it was a cell because there were bars on the window. But there were curtains he could pull closed to hide the bars. The bed was normal with clean sheets and a blanket and a pillow. The chair was normal. There was a small table with a normal lamp on it and some old American magazines. There was a toilet in the corner of the room. It was clean and it looked like it worked.

"Don't try to hurt yourself," said the guard, and removed the shackles. Zaharia rubbed his wrists and his ankles. "We'll be watching, so don't try to hurt yourself. All right?"

After a while a doctor came into the cell. He examined Zaharia's lip. He washed it off and put some salve on it. It burned a little. "Take off your shirt," he said. Zaharia did as he was told. The doctor touched and prodded Zaharia here and there wherever he saw bruises and some places he didn't. "Does this hurt? How about this?

"Stand up," said the doctor. "Raise your arms shoulder high." The doctor made a few notes. Then he did an extraordinary thing. He put his hand on Zaharia's shoulder and gave it a little rub, a small friendly gesture.

Zaharia sat on the edge of his bed and stared at the floor. He did not dare think what he wanted to think. He tried not to think anything. But somewhere in his mind he heard the silly voice of hope. It seemed to get louder and louder. Suddenly he could not see the floor anymore because his eyes had filled with tears. He lay facedown on the bed and wrapped the pillow around his face as though he wanted to smother himself. But he only wanted to smother the sobs.

Bobby was not eager to get involved in the drama Louis was planning. Neither was Jamal. He was a policeman after all, and he had already so overstepped the bounds of what was proper and legal for a Newark police officer, that if anyone on the force ever found out what he had done and, worse, what he was contemplating, he would go to jail for a very long time. The Greek chorus was even less eager than Bobby and Jamal. Who was this crazy old man anyway? They just stared at Louis hard-eyed as he talked and talked.

Finally the young man with EEK on his gold chain spoke. "Are you crazy, motherfucker?"

"Probably," said Louis.

EEK and his friends were on the verge of leaving. They had owed Jamal, but EEK figured now they were even. "Jamal, this isn't going to work. This goes way beyond making sense." What did Jamal need them for, EEK wondered. All there was, was to protect Fareed from one dopey CIA man. Jamal could do that by himself. Even over-the-hill Bobby could do it.

"He won't come alone," said Louis. "The CIA man. He'll say he's alone. But he won't be."

"So how many will there be?" said EEK.

"However many they think are enough," said Louis. That was the wrong answer.

"If they think you're alone, then one half man is enough," said EEK, and the rest of the Greek chorus snickered. "You be in touch, Jamal," said EEK. "When the time comes. Maybe we'll be there. To watch it happen." There would be guns. That was one thing. That was for sure. The CIA guys would have guns. Maybe EEK and his boys would take the CIA guns. That would be interesting. Louis was fairly certain it was all too strange and wild for them to resist.

* * *

Louis and Pauline had eaten dinner at La Colline next door to the Metropolitan Hotel. Louis had picked it to make it easy for Dimitrius to keep an eye on them. The place—a steak house—was pretentious, expensive, and ordinary, one of those establishments that favors fussy waiters, buttery sauces, and overcooked food. It didn't matter since neither he nor Pauline had much of an appetite.

Now they sat in their hotel room. The lights were off, but they had left the curtains of the big window open, and the room was lit up by the city. The buildings on the other side of the park twinkled and glimmered. The park itself lay in darkness, like a lagoon.

As Louis explained it to Pauline, his plan wasn't really much of a plan. If Peter Sanchez showed up with Zaharia, then Louis would allow Sanchez to debrief Fareed. Sanchez would want something he could check out right away, while they waited. It would have to prove Fareed's al Qaeda connection. Louis had yet to figure out what that would be. If the information checked out, Sanchez would then have to be persuaded to let Fareed leave with Louis. That was the tricky part.

"Persuaded," said Pauline.

"That's my preference," said Louis.

"Persuaded how?" said Pauline.

"He doesn't really need Fareed," said Louis. He shrugged. "I know that's not very persuasive. They always like having someone to show off to the media, someone to lock up and punish. So I'm not hopeful. That's why it's important that we have Jamal along, and especially his friends. They're liable to be good at persuasion."

"You mean intimidation." Pauline tried to study Louis's face, but it was hidden in shadow. "Sometimes you're different than I thought you were," she said.

"Do I frighten you?" said Louis.

"No," said Pauline. "Of course not. But I think you must frighten yourself."

Louis gazed from the hotel window. "I don't know what came first," he said. "My secret self or my secret career."

"Your secret self?" said Pauline.

"The part I keep hidden," said Louis.

"The part you *imagine* you keep hidden," said Pauline. "I don't think you keep very much hidden. But you try. You're lonelier than you need to be." She reached into the shadows and touched his cheek.

"You're different too," said Louis. He turned and looked at Pauline. Her face was lit up by the city.

"Different how?" said Pauline. "Different from what?"

"Different from . . . what I thought I wanted."

Pauline smiled. "And what did you think you wanted?"

"I thought I wanted to be alone."

Later, they lay in bed. Pauline lay with her head on Louis's arm. Both were lost in their thoughts. Finally Louis spoke. "There's still our wild card to figure out."

"Our wild card?"

"Phillip Dimitrius. What's he up to? How will he figure in at the end? He's clumsy, but I don't think he's stupid. Although in his business it comes down to the same thing. Still, I think he must know something of where we've been and what we've been up to."

"How?" said Pauline.

"He probably followed us. We lost him the first day. But I'm sure he didn't let that happen again."

"Does that mean that Sanchez knows what you're up to?"

"That's a good question," said Louis.

At that very moment, Phillip Dimitrius was sitting in the bar in La Colline peering at the world through a crystal snifter of cognac. Each time he took a sip, the room turned golden. Phillip had a slightly goofy smile that he never displayed. But just now, he allowed himself a brief congratulatory grin. The curtain was about to rise on the next act. His long pursuit of Louis Morgon was about to bear fruit, and plenty of it.

Phillip believed in the war on terror, in the conflict between good and evil, all those things, in a way Peter Sanchez, for instance, did not. Peter's understanding of things was clouded by his ambition and what he probably would have called his nuanced sense of things. Lord knew what Louis Morgon believed in his addled, sick brain.

But Phillip Dimitrius, the child of hard-working immigrants who had been welcomed by the great United States, knew about the heart and soul of America. He had a clearer sense of things than Sanchez or his ilk. His understanding was hard and unwavering. It was, put succinctly, that the United States was a force for good, a beacon that everyone in the world should follow, *must* follow if the world was going to survive. And if only everyone would get behind that vision, then order would ensue and everything would finally fall into its rightful place. Phillip was not a fool. He knew that he had little power. His talents were limited. He was neither brilliant nor astute. But he was dogged and intrepid. He was a worker in the America factory, a tiller of the soil of freedom. And that was all he needed to be sure of, in order to forge ahead in his intrepid way. He closed his eyes and took another sip of the brandy.

Now Phillip thought he knew several things for certain. For one, Louis Morgon was a terrorist. If he wasn't actually al Qaeda himself, then he damn sure was an al Qaeda hand-maiden. Phillip had followed his trail through Algeria and Cairo and Paris where Morgon had made one Qaeda linkup after another. Now, thanks in large part to Phillip, one prospective terrorist—Zaharia Lefort—was in prison. And another—Fareed Terzani—was cornered in Newark and about to meet the full righteous fury of the American justice system.

And the biggest prize of all—Louis Morgon—had come to Newark. He was finally on American soil where they could take him. The only conclusion Phillip could draw was that they—Fareed, Louis, the rest of them, whoever they were—were planning an event on American soil. Another 9/11 maybe. There were enough people involved for Phillip to conclude with a fair degree of certitude—as he had told his FBI contacts—something spectacular was planned. Phillip had worked the whole thing out and lined up his quarry in his sights while Peter Sanchez was off dithering around Cairo.

Phillip Dimitrius had come to the CIA from the FBI. Phillip had always believed—just like the president and the homeland security director—that there was too little communication between security agencies. After all, they were fighting the same enemies, weren't they? Talking to one another, sharing intelligence, cooperating on raids and prosecutions could only enhance what the FBI director liked to call "the security landscape."

Phillip had coordinated carefully with his FBI contacts, and, when the moment was right, they had picked up Zaharia Lefort. It had been done neatly and with a minimum of fuss. And, according to all reports, the interrogation of Lefort had borne fruit. Fareed Terzani and Louis Morgon were next. "They're going down," was how Phillip Dimitrius put it. "All of them."

Special agents were convening in the Manhattan office of the FBI. Fax machines were humming into the night as intelligence reports, mug shots, maps, and diagrams went whizzing about. Computers were busily uploading and downloading warrants, indictments, and any other piece of paper deemed, by one agent or another, to be essential to the operation. Blue protective vests, with FBI printed in enormous yellow block letters on the back, hung at the ready. Automatic weapons were cleaned and oiled and resting in their racks.

"Another Courvoisier, sir?" said the bartender.

"Better not," said Phillip. "Big day tomorrow."

XVI

Zaharia was taken from his cell, put in a van, and driven across the city of Newark. He did not think he had ever heard of Newark before, unless it was in a geography class. He had not been told where he was going. But as they drove across the city's ruined industrial quarter, along canals with oily junk floating in them, past collapsed buildings and other assorted ruination—houses without windows or doors, piles of garbage, junked cars and appliances, burnt-out tractor trailers, and a few wrecked people too—Zaharia thought, *This is a deadly place.* It was true that they had just treated him humanely for the first time since he had been arrested. It did not seem possible they would choose to kill him now. But he could not let go of the thought. *This is where they take you to kill you*, said the voice of despair.

The van stopped inside the remains of a concrete garage, a great, gray space with a low ceiling. The only light came from the door they had come through and from a jagged opening at the far end of the building where a ramp to the next level had crumbled away and taken a section of wall with it. Chunks of concrete dangled from twisted, rusting bars of iron.

Zaharia and the guard escorting him got out of the van and walked toward the ruined ramp. Some men were standing there in the shadows. For a moment Zaharia did not recognize Louis Morgon. But then he did recognize him. Zaharia's wrist was shackled to a guard's, so he could not rush forward. "Take off the shackles," said Louis. Another man signaled to the guard, who removed the shackles from his wrists. Louis walked up to Zaharia and the two embraced. Louis felt a sob rise in the boy's body.

"Are you all right?" said Louis.

"Yes," said Zaharia.

"Zaharia," said Louis, "this is Bobby. He's going to take you home with him. I will see you there later. You'll be safe."

Bobby nodded. "You'll be safe at my house," he said. Zaharia and Bobby left the ruined garage. They drove back to Keyser Street. "Here we are," said Bobby. "That door sticks.

You have to kick it." Zaharia gave the Cadillac door a mighty kick and the door jumped open. "Damn!" said Bobby.

Zaharia laughed. He almost couldn't stop laughing.

"Come on in," said Bobby. He held the gate. Junior rushed out to greet them. "Get down, Junior," said Bobby.

Lillian was waiting inside. "I'm Lillian," she said. "This is Pauline. And this is Natalie. Louis will be back soon. Come have something to eat. You like pizza?"

"Yes," said Zaharia. "I love pizza."

Louis presented Fareed to Peter Sanchez. Peter looked Fareed up and down. Then he looked at Jamal. "Who's this?"

"He's a Newark police officer," said Louis.

"You were supposed to come alone," said Peter. "The arrangement was just you and Fareed."

"And you were supposed to come alone," said Louis.

"This is my driver and one other agent," said Peter. "I can't take Fareed into custody by myself."

"And who are the men hidden outside?" said Louis. He pointed in various directions.

Peter gave Louis a long look. He turned back to Fareed. "Let's see what you've got," he said finally. "Give me something I can check."

"Did you bring your computer like I said?" said Louis.

Peter Sanchez held up a small instrument the size of a

calculator. Louis looked at Fareed, and Fareed nodded. "It's a BlackBerry," said Fareed, and Louis shrugged. The world had passed him by.

Louis opened the small plastic portfolio he was carrying and withdrew a page, which he handed to Peter. "It's a Web address," said Fareed. "A log-in and a series of passwords. Try them and see what you get." Peter handed the BlackBerry to one of the agents, who poked at the tiny keyboard with his thumbs, waited, poked some more, waited, poked some more, and waited again. When the screen finally came to life he passed the BlackBerry to Peter Sanchez. "What is it?" said Peter.

"I don't know exactly," said the agent. "Numbers. Arabic numerals."

"What is it?" Peter Sanchez said to Fareed.

"It is a series of codes, the current codes for access to a Qaeda Web site."

"What's on the Web site?" Peter wanted to know.

Fareed looked at Louis and Louis nodded. "It is for those who want to train with al Qaeda," he said. "It gives you— them—the first step in the procedure for getting to a training camp."

"Does it give the second step?" said Peter. "And the third?" Peter looked at the BlackBerry as though he might be holding a scorpion in his hand.

"Try it," said Louis.

Peter gave the BlackBerry and the list of numbers back to

the agent. The agent poked in the codes. He was taken to a site with text in several languages, including English, about the necessity of Holy War. It mentioned satanic regimes around the world. "This is bullshit," said the agent.

"Punch in the next code," said Fareed, pointing to the bottom of the sheet of paper. When the agent punched in the numbers and letters, a screen came up directing Holy Warriors to a particular address in the city of Islamabad, Pakistan. "That's the start of the chain that took me to Osama bin Laden," said Fareed.

"The start of the chain," said Peter.

"It wasn't on the Internet then, and the address changes, but it worked the same way. One person sent you to the next. You go to Islamabad to learn the next step. The codes and addresses are always changing. And the code to get the codes changes too. Depending on security."

Peter looked at the BlackBerry. "It's something, but it's not much," he said.

"You'll get the rest," said Louis.

"We'll take Fareed and interrogate him," said Peter. He signaled the two agents, who stepped toward Fareed.

"If you take Fareed now, there's a good chance you've gotten everything you're going to get. If you let him leave with me—leave here and leave the country—you'll get the whole jackpot. The code to get the code changes. Plus active Qaeda cells in Newark, in New York City, in Bridgeport, Connecticut.

You'll get addresses, telephone numbers, and codes that they'll accept, codes that will mark you as al Qaeda. Later on you'll get even more."

"You're crazy," said Peter. "There's no way I'm letting him walk out of here with you."

"Let me put it another way," said Louis. "If you try to take him, you'll have to take me too, or kill me. And, as I'm sure you already know, I've made provisions for that eventuality. In that moment, the moment of his arrest and/or mine, all the information I just summarized, the whole catalog of Fareed's knowledge, will be on its way to reporters at *The New York Times, The Washington Post*, and a number of other newspapers and Internet and television outlets. It's a big story, so it will be public knowledge within a matter of hours. The envelopes are sealed, addressed, postage is attached. All that's missing is a signal from me, or rather the *absence* of a signal from me, to send them on their way."

"Jesus H. Christ, Louis. Do you even understand the meaning of treason anymore?"

"You know," said Louis. "I don't think I do. Maybe you could explain it to me."

Louis waited while Peter collected himself. "All right," said Peter finally. "How do we get everything he's got?"

Louis took out an envelope from inside his coat and handed it to Peter. "Here's the essence of it. Study it. Call me with questions."

Peter looked doubtful. "Look in the envelope," said Louis.

Everything that Louis said would be there was there—
Qaeda cells all over the New York area, as well as other information about foiled plots and misfired plots and plots that had never gotten off the ground. Peter kept looking up at Fareed, as the measure of his own good fortune dawned on him.

"All right," said Peter. "You're free to go." But it was Peter who turned and left, reading the papers as he walked. As he and the two agents walked out of the garage, a dozen other agents, who had been stationed outside, joined them. The Greek chorus emerged from their hiding places and watched them go.

"I can't believe it," said Fareed. "Am I really free? I can't believe it."

"So, are we finished?" said Jamal.

"Maybe. For the moment anyway," said Louis. "Let's go back to Keyser Street. Call Bobby and tell him. Everyone will be anxious to hear from us."

Jamal poked at his cell phone. "Hey, Bobby . . . Yeah, man. How's everything there? . . . What? . . . Pizza?" Jamal hung up the phone. He had a puzzled look on his face.

"What was that all about?" said Louis.

"I don't know. It was weird."

"Tell me," said Louis.

"Bobby said some weird shit."

"Tell me exactly what he said."

"Well, first he asked me if everything was all right. So I said yes. Then I asked him how things were there, and he said Junior was fine."

"Junior?" said Louis. "The dog?"

"Yeah. Then he said they were all waiting for us, eating pizza. He talked about how Junior loves his pizza."

"All right, Jamal. Take me back to Bobby's. Then take Fareed someplace safe and wait for my call."

"What is it?" said Jamal.

"I think Bobby's warning us that something's wrong. Somebody's there."

"Somebody's there? Who?"

"I can only think of one person."

An hour earlier Phillip Dimitrius had gotten in the lead car of the FBI convoy—two cars followed by two vans. He gave the signal and they sped down the turnpike and across Newark. The cars turned up Keyser Street and jammed on their brakes, blocking the street in both directions. The vans drove up the alley behind Bobby and Lillian's house and stopped. Everyone piled out. There were twenty men in all, wearing blue FBI ball caps and blue FBI vests over their Kevlar body armor. They carried shotguns, tear gas grenades, and stun guns. Several men had packs on their backs with other equipment in them— radios, first-aid equipment, gas masks, plastic handcuffs.

Junior came running up to greet them. He looked like he might bark, so everybody burst in through the front and back doors. Lillian screamed. Bobby jumped up, but two FBI men grabbed him and slammed him back onto his chair. Zaharia did not move, but two men restrained him as well. They withdrew plastic handcuffs from the packs and secured everyone's hands—including Lillian, Pauline, and Natalie—behind their backs where they sat. They searched the house. They stood by each doorway with their backs pressed against the wall, finally lunging through the door and shouting, "Clear!" *Just like on television,* thought Bobby.

"Where's Louis Morgon?" said Phillip Dimitrius.

"He's not here," said Bobby.

"You expect him back?" said Dimitrius.

"I don't know," said Bobby.

"Where's Fareed?" said Dimitrius.

"Who?" said Bobby.

"Oh, Lord," said Lillian.

Phillip turned to Lillian. "Where's Fareed?"

"Lord, I don't know," she said.

"When's he coming back?"

"I don't know when he's coming back."

Phillip huddled with some of the FBI men. They laid a trap for Louis and Fareed. First the cars and vans were removed from sight. Then the FBI people dispersed themselves. They hid in yards, between houses, in the muffler shop, beside Louie's Pizza, and up and down the alley. They shooed away any curious onlookers.

Phillip turned back to his prisoners. "You people are in big trouble," he said. "Now's the time to do what you can to help yourselves. Anybody?" Bobby glared at Phillip with such ferocity that Phillip had to look away. "All right then," he said to no one in particular. He pulled a chair to the front window. "We'll just wait."

Bobby's phone rang. Phillip took the phone. He made a note of the incoming number. "Who's that?" he asked Bobby. Bobby looked at the screen. "Jamal," he said. "Lillian's boy."

"Answer it. Tell him to come back." Phillip held the phone to Bobby's ear in such a way that he could hear both sides of the conversation. Bobby did as he was told.

"Stop, Jamal. Let me out here," said Louis. "Any closer to the house and they might have a perimeter set up. Take Fareed somewhere safe and wait." Louis got out by a bridge across the canal. It was still six blocks to Bobby and Lillian's. The streets were empty.

Louis walked up Keyser Street. He looked straight ahead. He didn't see the FBI. He didn't need to. He knew they were there. At Bobby's house he opened the gate and Junior rushed up to greet him. Louis smiled and patted Junior's big head. "Hi, Junior," he said.

When Louis walked through the front door, agents were waiting with their guns drawn. Louis was made to sit on a chair. His hands were restrained behind the chair back with PlastiCuffs. Phillip Dimitrius stood over Louis. "Are you Louis Morgon?"

"I am," said Louis. "And you must be Phillip Dimitrius."

"That's none of your business . . ."

"Do you have Peter Sanchez's telephone number?"

"What?" said Phillip.

"Peter Sanchez's phone number. Do you have it? You should probably give him a call."

XVII

With only a little more persuasion from Louis—a mention of the very real possibility of an article in *The New York Times*—Phillip Dimitrius called Peter Sanchez. Phillip told Peter that he and the FBI had three terror suspects in custody.

"Who?" Peter wondered.

Phillip named them. Louis Morgon, Fareed Terzani, Zaharia Lefort. He added that he had also arrested others who appeared to be accomplices.

There was a long silence at the other end of the line. Then Peter Sanchez instructed Phillip Dimitrius to release everyone. Immediately. Peter sounded reasonably calm, so Phillip decided to press his case.

"Release Louis Morgon?" he said.

"Yes," said Peter.

"Fareed Terzani? He's a . . ."

"*Everyone,*" said Peter. "Release *everyone.*"

"I'm going to need a written authorization for the release," said Phillip.

Again there was a long silence. "What you're going to need," said Peter, and this time his voice was not as calm, "is a written authorization for arresting them in the first place. Otherwise the next *written authorization* you see will be for your removal from service. And that will be followed by other *written authorizations* you don't even want to think about."

Phillip Dimitrius hung up the phone. He and the FBI agents used clippers to remove everyone's PlastiCuffs. They packed away all their weapons and other equipment, and left the house without saying a word. Junior rushed up to greet them as they stepped off the porch. They even ignored Junior.

Lillian and Bobby went outside and watched them walk down Keyser Street. Agents came from all over to join the exodus. "Damn!" said Bobby.

"Would you look at that," said Lillian.

Louis and Pauline and Fareed and Natalie and Zaharia flew back to Paris together. Louis insisted on that.

In the plane, Pauline gazed out the window.

"I apologize," said Louis.

Pauline looked at him for a long moment. "For what?"

"For everything," said Louis.

"Everything?" she said. "That is too easy. If you're going to apologize, it has to be for something."

They cleared customs in Paris without difficulty. Even Fareed. He and Natalie took the RER train from the airport and then switched to the bus for Clichy-sous-Bois. Louis wondered whether he would ever see them again.

"Shall we share a taxi to Montparnasse?" said Louis.

"I'd rather not," said Pauline.

"Does she blame you?" said Zaharia.

"I don't know," said Louis.

"It wasn't your fault," said Zaharia. "It was all a mistake." Where had this boy come from that he could be so forgiving?

"Let's go home, Zaharia. We need to make arrangements to get you home to your granny."

"Will I be able to go back to Potomac School?"

"You still want to do that?" said Louis.

"Yes," said Zaharia. "I was learning to play basketball. I liked my life there. I liked living with Jennifer. And seeing Michael and Rosita. I liked my friends. I liked my classes."

"But are you sure you want to go back?" said Louis.

"It wasn't America's fault. It wasn't anybody's fault. It was just a bad mistake."

"Maybe you can go back. We'll look into it. But first let's go to Saint Leon for a few days. I'll rest up, and then I'll take you home. How does that sound?"

It took a week before Louis felt strong enough to travel again. He was not sorry that it took that long. Being in Zaharia's company healed Louis's exhausted spirit. He watched as the boy searched through his library, pulling out one book, then putting it back, doing it again and again, until he found something he could get lost in. He would settle into the corner of the collapsed sofa and read and read and read.

Louis and Zaharia took a walk every morning. "It will be good for you," said Louis. But mainly it was good for Louis. Just to walk with the boy beside him.

"Does someone live in that chateau?" Zaharia asked.

"The Beaumonts do," said Louis. "They have other houses too. Sometime, when they're in town and you're here too, I'll ask if we can visit. They have wonderful old barns, from the sixteenth and seventeenth centuries. With beams this thick." He spread his arms. "And their caves. Some of their caves are so deep no one knows where they end."

"Will Pauline come back down to see you?" said Zaharia.

"To see her daughter," said Louis.

"To see you?" said Zaharia.

"Maybe," said Louis. "I don't know."

"If she doesn't," said Zaharia, "then you should go to Paris and see her."

Louis and Zaharia flew to Algiers together. Louis waited with his old friend Samad at the Hôtel de Boufa while Moamar delivered Zaharia to his grandmother. "I am only staying one night," he told Samad. "I'll come back again soon for a longer stay."

"When you are stronger," said Samad. "You don't look well."

"Thank you for noticing," said Louis.

"It is the least I can do," said Samad. Both men laughed.

On his way home Louis called Pauline from Charles de Gaulle airport. He wondered whether they could meet. Pauline hesitated and then agreed. "I'll make you dinner," she said. She did not invite him to stay the night. She broiled some tuna and made a tomato and white bean confit. They ate mostly in silence.

"An experience like the one we had seems to change every-thing," said Pauline finally. They were drinking coffee and eating the last bites of a chocolate tart.

"I don't know why it does," said Louis. "But I knew it would."

"You even warned me," she said.

"Yes," said Louis. "I warned you. But I don't understand it. I don't know. What exactly has it changed?"

"I'm not certain," said Pauline. "I couldn't name one thing. And yet everything feels different. The world, this apartment, you, us. I'm different now. Having someone follow you, point guns at you, handcuff you, all that changes you."

"You thought the world was one way, and it turns out to be another way," said Louis.

"Yes, that's for sure," said Pauline. "But I also thought you were one way and you turned out . . . different."

"Ah," said Louis.

"Not like you're thinking," she said. "You didn't suddenly go from being gentle to being violent or anything like that. But you became more . . . an enigma. A mystery. An unsolvable puzzle. You're smiling."

"Because," said Louis, "I couldn't possibly be more of an enigma to you than I am to myself."

"We all do things, think things that are mysterious to ourselves. But you have a subterranean life, a part of you that comes to the surface and then disappears," said Pauline.

"A subterranean life?"

"Your history, I guess. Your history barges into your life. I think I was fine while it remained history. I simply could not imagine that a man's past could so thoroughly take over his present."

"It is a kind of curse," said Louis.

"An occupational curse?" said Pauline.

"Not always," said Louis. "Most spies are allowed to retire and lead quiet, boring lives. I just happened to make the wrong enemy—Hugh Bowes—long ago, and that started a long chain of events that took me over. Not by my choosing, but it took me over nonetheless."

"I don't know, Louis. That sounds like an excuse. What 'curse'? Enemies? It sounds like a way of letting yourself off the hook."

"Does it?" said Louis. "But there is always the possibility of something . . ."

"And that is what I don't know about," said Pauline. "Can I stand that?"

"Waiting for the other shoe to drop?" said Louis.

"No, not waiting. Knowing that *you're* waiting. That you're keeping a part of yourself in reserve for the moment when the other shoe drops. That's what poisons everything. Even love. That waiting."

"It doesn't have to," said Louis. "It shouldn't." He thought for a moment. "There is always the chance," he said, as though it were a new idea, "that there is no other shoe. And even if there is another shoe, if I can live without . . . expectations . . ."

"Without expectations? Who can live without expectations?" said Pauline. "I'll walk with you to the train."

They walked in silence. It was a blustery night. A few snowflakes were swirling around. You couldn't see them in the shadows. Only in the aura around streetlamps and in front of shop windows. But you knew they were everywhere. Louis felt them on his face. Louis and Pauline walked close together against the cold.

At the Montparnasse station, Pauline kissed his cheek. "Thank you for coming," she said.

He touched her arm. She walked away. On the train he stared at the window, but all he saw was his own face.

*　*　*

It was the first day of spring. A soft, warm breeze ruffled the scalloped edge of the umbrellas on the terrace at the Hôtel de France. Daffodils and jonquils had come up in the beds around the square. A few were in bloom. They tossed their heads in the breeze, like young girls.

Louis loosened the collar of his coat and shifted his chair so the sun shone on his back. "Peter Sanchez called," he said.

"Really?" said Renard.

"In a perverse way, it's a hopeful sign," said Louis. "It tells me we're not enemies. I would not want him as my enemy."

A waiter came over, a young man with a blond cowlick.

"Coffee," said Renard.

"Tea," said Louis. "Do you have chamomile?"

"*Oui, monsieur,*" said the waiter.

"Chamomile then," said Louis. He watched the waiter go. "A new waiter?"

"Albert," said Renard. "Chamomile tea?"

"Doctor's orders. One of François's precautions." The two men waited in silence for their drinks to come.

"And why did Peter Sanchez call?" said Renard.

"To thank me," said Louis.

"You're kidding," said Renard.

Louis had been working on a self-portrait, just drawing in the rough edges of the head, when the phone rang. "It's Peter Sanchez," said the voice at the other end.

"Is that your real name?" said Louis.

Peter laughed. "I called to thank you," he said.

"That I made you a hero?" said Louis.

"Something like that," said Peter. "But mostly because you were straight with me. Everything you gave me was good. Everything checked out."

"That was Fareed," said Louis. "You should thank him."

"We closed down two cells," said Peter.

"I saw it in the paper," said Louis.

"And we're working on others. They gave up other people. We stopped some seriously nasty business before it happened. That wasn't in the paper."

"Were they tortured?" said Louis.

"We don't torture people," said Peter. He didn't laugh.

"What happened to Phillip Dimitrius?" said Louis.

"That hasn't been decided," said Peter.

"Why don't you promote him?" said Louis.

"Promote him?"

"He might do less damage that way," said Louis.

"Good-bye, Louis," said Peter. He hung up the phone.

Renard stirred his coffee. "And *is* Peter Sanchez his real name?"

"I tried to call him back, just out of curiosity. I got a recorded message saying the number is not in use."

Renard took a sip of coffee. He looked out across the square. "So," he said. They sat in silence for a while. Then: "And what did François say?"

Louis took a sip of tea. "He said I'm the worst patient he's ever had."

"Which you took as a compliment."

"Of course."

"And the cancer?"

"Is gone."

"Really?"

"Really."

"That's wonderful news," said Renard.

"But the tests . . ."

"Please," said Renard. "Don't start on that with me." He signaled for the check.

The two men sat in silence. "You still haven't talked to Pauline?"

"No," said Louis.

"I've got to get back," said Renard. He stood up. "Gerard Saint Colombe, do you know him? He got drunk last night and put Jules Nevière in the hospital."

Pauline called in April. "I want to see you," she said.

"Really?" said Louis. He heard the silly voice of hope inside his head. Zaharia had told him about the silly voice of hope. "I'm coming to Saint Leon. I'm bringing someone to meet you," she said.

"Who," said Louis.

"Wait and see," said Pauline.

The day was sunny but chilly. A north wind blew hard along the station platform so that Louis had to turn up his collar and pull his hat down to keep the dust out of his eyes. He watched Pauline get off the train. She wore a down jacket. She had walking shoes on her feet and carried her small backpack over one shoulder. Then Fareed and Natalie got off behind her. Fareed was carrying a basket. Pauline kissed Louis. Natalie kissed Louis. So did Fareed.

Fareed held the basket while Natalie pulled the blankets aside to reveal a baby, a tiny, new baby with thick black hair and large black eyes. "This is Louise," said Natalie.

"Really?" said Louis. "Louise?"

"Really."